Murder Is Legal

A Susan Wiles Schoolhouse Mystery

by

Diane Weiner

For information, email Cozy Cat Press, cozycatpress@aol.com or visit our website at: www.cozycatpress.com

COZY CAT
P R E S S

ISBN: 978-1-939816-90-0
Printed in the United States of America

Cover design by Paula Ellenberger
http://www.paulaellenberger.com/

10 9 8 7 6 5 4 3 2 1

This book is dedicated to my father, Joachim Grigull. He read every one of my books and was one of my strongest cheerleaders. His absence is greatly missed.

Chapter 1

The letter. If she'd never received the letter, she'd be at home on her couch watching Dr. Oz right now instead of sitting in this beehive of traffic approaching Kennedy Airport. After all, now that she was retired and her husband, Mike, had lightened his workload after his recent heart attack, they were flying in the middle of the day, in the middle of the workweek, and in the middle of autumn—no long weekend or holiday in sight. Susan Wiles peacefully napped in the front seat during the two-hour drive from their home in the small town of Westbrook, New York, but the fits and starts of the traffic now jarred her awake. She rubbed her eyes.

"Are we there yet?"

"Almost," answered Mike.

Mike drove around in circles, hunting down a spot in the nearly full parking garage. Susan's patience was already waning, and they'd barely started their journey.

Her neck muscles ached as they wheeled their carry-on bags to a security line that snaked through the automatic doors out to the sidewalk.

"I hate flying," said Susan.

Mike responded, "It was your idea to cancel our cruise and go to Atlanta."

"We'll still do the cruise. It's merely been postponed. You know I couldn't ignore *the letter*."

"Of course you couldn't. I'm telling you, curiosity killed the cat as they say. You have no idea what we may be walking into. You don't even know who sent it. Good thing you have me by your side."

Susan gave him a light swat on the arm. "I do know who sent it. Mr. Brooks B. Churchill."

"And you really haven't a clue who Brooks B. Churchill is. We've been over this."

The plane boarded. Susan wheeled the bag beside her like a dog on a leash, thankful she'd recently replaced her old luggage that had a haywire wheel. Now in her early sixties, she felt the occasional stiff muscle and pretended not to hear the creaky sound her knees sometimes made when she stood up after sitting too long.

"You know I'm always supportive of you, and I agreed to make this trip, but I'm worried about you. I think it's mighty fishy how you got that letter asking you to come to Atlanta just after you discovered your birth father lives there. Like I said earlier, don't be surprised if the letter is somehow connected to him. Be prepared if that's the case."

"This has nothing to do with Jonathan Stirling. He's on sabbatical in England."

Susan had ridden an emotional roller coaster ever since her mom, the woman she'd assumed was her birth mom, had died. Susan was shocked to find adoption papers in her deceased mom's safety deposit box. Reeling from the discovery that she was adopted, she set about finding her birth mother, Audrey Roberts.

Audrey ran a private performing arts high school in Florida. Susan, Susan's daughter, and her granddaughter made a recent trip to Banyan Beach to meet her. Just when she was bonding with Audrey (while solving a teacher's murder and nailing a drug ring), she'd found out that Audrey had concealed the identity of her birth father. The "fasten seat belt" sign came on again just as turbulence nearly propelled Susan into the aisle.

"I'd understand if this was about meeting your birth father."

"Audrey said my father was a summer fling who she never saw again."

"But in fact it was her boyfriend at the time— Jonathan Stirling. Jonathan never knew she was pregnant. He still doesn't know he has a daughter. I totally support you reconnecting with him. What I don't understand is why you feel compelled to meet Brooks Churchill if you believe he has nothing to do with your father," said Mike. "Oh yes, *the letter*. 'Unique talent for solving puzzles… a personal benefit to be gained…' A cryptic piece of mumbo jumbo if you ask me."

Susan and Mike had discussed the letter and whether or not to make the trip to Atlanta at length. In the end, after over forty years of marriage, Mike knew Susan's stubbornness and curiosity wouldn't allow her to ignore the letter.

"It's not like we have more urgent issues to tend to. Besides, it'll be a nice getaway. The Braves are in the play-off. I know you can't wait to see the game I got tickets to."

"Yeah, well… talk about bribery." Mike looked out the window. "There it is. Hartsfield-Jackson Airport."

The landing was anything but smooth, and Susan was thankful she'd eaten lightly. They made their way off the plane and onto the tram that connected the terminals.

"The letter said this would prove to be a rewarding endeavor. Maybe we stand to inherit money. Audrey grew up in Atlanta. Maybe some distant relative named me in his will."

"The only people from Atlanta who knew you existed are Audrey, her long-deceased parents, and Richard Stirling, Jonathan's brother. Richard's sitting in a jail cell back in New York. He killed his wife, remember? No money's coming from him."

"I sincerely hope Audrey has gotten over her infatuation with Richard Stirling by now. Visiting him in jail? Paying for additional defense lawyers to reopen his case? How does an intelligent, professional woman like Audrey get duped like that?"

They exited the tram and rode the longest escalator Susan had ever seen. "Want to take MARTA or a taxi? MARTA is cheaper," said Mike.

"I just want to get to our hotel and relax before our meeting. I vote for a taxi."

The cab circumvented the city traffic, and after a hilly ride on Interstate 285, they cruised through suburbs so sumptuous Susan's mouth watered. She gushed over the Tudor-style stone houses and the spacious brick ones. The fall foliage was at its peak just as it was at home in the Hudson Valley. They passed a health-food store, an assortment of restaurants, and a Barnes & Noble.

"Look, there's Iberton University," said Susan. Iberton University looked like the campus Harry Potter attended. The gothic buildings were majestic, and it was surrounded by manicured grounds sprinkled with crinkled, colored leaves. "It's smaller than I'd pictured."

"But looks charming."

At their hotel, Susan placed her neatly folded clothes into the drawers, kicked off her Easy Spirit mules, and stretched out on the bed. Mike went down the hall to the vending machines and brought back two cans of Coca Cola—Atlanta's official drink.

"Here you go." He handed Susan a Diet Coke. "You know, it's not too late to ditch the meeting and spend the afternoon at the aquarium."

Susan briefly considered Mike's suggestion, but the intrigue of the mysterious letter drew her in like a magnet. She closed her eyes and dozed off until it was time to get going. She changed into black pants and a baby-blue cashmere sweater that matched her eyes. Butterflies fluttered in her stomach. *What if Mike is right? What am I walking into? What if this Brooks guy is another Craigslist killer?* It wouldn't be the first time Susan's curiosity and impulsivity sucked her smack into the middle of danger.

Chapter 2

Holding hands, Susan and Mike walked the short distance to Iberton University. Encountering an increasing number of backpack-adorned millennials carrying Starbucks cups signaled their proximity. Densely packed trees lined the walkways. Following a campus map, Susan and Mike scanned the stone buildings and located the law school, which looked out of place with its long glass windows and brick exterior.

"Here we are," said Mike. "The library conference rooms are on the third floor."

Susan squeezed Mike's hand during the elevator ride. Her knees were shaking.

"We don't have to do this," said Mike.

Susan took a deep breath. "Come on, let's go in." They went to a conference room in the back of the library and were greeted by an elderly gentleman with curly, blond hair. He wore wire-rimmed glasses just like Susan's.

Extending his hand, he said, "I'm Brooks Churchill. I'm so grateful you came." Susan had insisted they meet in a public place. "As a paralegal, I spend many hours in this library. I had no trouble reserving a room here." Brooks spoke with a southern drawl, which Susan found charming. "Have a seat."

Brooks began. "Like I said in my letter…"

The conference room door opened, and Susan jumped to her feet. She felt her blood boiling under her mop of dirty-blond hair. "Audrey! What are you doing here? How dare you? I told you I never wanted to see you again." Susan turned to Brooks. "You tricked me. Audrey set this whole thing up, didn't she? We're leaving. Come on, Mike." She was blocked by Audrey, her birth mother, awkwardly positioned in front of the exit.

"Susan? I'm as surprised to see you as you are to see me. I got a letter..." She turned to Brooks. "What is this all about? You said you needed my help. You didn't say anything about my daughter being involved." Her words were angry and sharp.

"Now, ladies, have a seat." Brooks sat at the conference table out of the line of fire. "We're expecting one more person."

Susan glared at Audrey. Audrey diverted her eyes. In unison, both women said "Who?"

Right on cue, the conference room door swung open. Standing before them was a Clint Eastwood doppelganger. His wrinkle-framed eyes were as clear and blue as pool water.

Audrey awkwardly fidgeted with her hands.

Brooks turned to Susan and Mike and said, "I'd like to introduce you to Jonathan Stirling. Jonathan, Susan and Mike Wiles from New York. Audrey, you know each other, though I believe it's been quite some time since you were in contact."

Audrey's face turned the color of chalk.

Susan braced herself against the conference table in an attempt to avoid fainting. *Jonathan Stirling! I am face to face with my birth father. My birth father!* The words boomeranged through her head. He was supposed to be in Europe. *I'm not prepared for this.* Mike stood up and put his arm around her waist.

Jonathan extended his hand. With a smooth, southern accent, he said, "Nice to meet you." He turned to Audrey. Clearing his throat, he said, "How have you been? It's been a long time."

Susan noted Audrey's stiff jaw and tightly drawn smile lines when she looked at Jonathan. Jonathan had no idea Audrey had been pregnant. Richard Stirling, Jonathan's brother, had confirmed that when she visited him at Bayersville State Correctional Institute back in New York. Jonathan was naïve to the fact that his flesh-and-blood daughter was standing before him. Now, for the first time ever, the whole family was together in the same room. *This is unreal,* thought Susan. Audrey shot Susan a sideways glance. Susan read mountains in her expression. With her hand blocking Jonathan's view, Audrey mouthed the words *don't tell him.*

Susan grabbed Mike's hand. "We're leaving now."

"No," said Brooks. "Please hear me out. Have a seat. You'll want to hear what I'm going to say." Susan looked at Mike, who simply shrugged his shoulders. She looked at the door, then at Audrey and Jonathan. Reluctantly she sat down.

Brooks began. "As you are all aware, thanks to Susan and her detective daughter, my old friend Richard Stirling has been granted a new trial."

Audrey's face tightened. "*I'm* the one who insisted we take a second look at Richard's case."

Brooks continued, "Yes, of course. And Audrey." He flashed Audrey a toothy smile. Susan wondered if he'd had those sixtyish-year-old teeth professionally whitened. "I received new information from a private investigator. He found a witness who swears he saw a green van in the Stirling's driveway the night Maggie Stirling was murdered."

"We knew that," said Susan. "My daughter wasn't able to connect with him."

"I *have*," said Brooks. "I've set up a meeting for all of us."

"Why are you so interested in this case?" said Susan.

"Richard and I grew up together. We all did." He looked from Jonathan to Audrey. "Richard's like a brother to me. He saved my life. When I was forced to leave law school, he got me a job up in New York. I owe him."

Susan noticed Jonathan's scowl as he spoke up. "I don't understand why you called me here. My brother is guilty as sin. I've known it since the day we found out Maggie was dead thirty years ago. We all know it."

Jonathan, Richard's own brother, believes he killed his wife, Susan said to herself. He must know him better than anyone.

"That's not true," said Audrey. "Richard is innocent."

"It sure as heck *is* true. Richard went bowling with his buddies to establish an alibi, then snuck back into his own house through the garage door and bludgeoned his wife to death with a fireplace poker," said Brooks.

"Why would he do that?" asked Audrey. "Richard isn't capable of that degree of violence. Besides, he loved his wife. He had nothing to gain by killing her."

"Maggie wanted a divorce, and she wanted half the company Richard founded," said Jonathan.

"That doesn't mean…," said Audrey.

"Come on. Richard wouldn't stand for it. He's my brother. I know how he thinks," said Jonathan.

Audrey crossed her arms tightly over her chest like a stubborn child. "There's no proof. We discovered the evidence had been tampered with."

Susan jumped into the exchange. "There was a missing glove, and no one talked to the eyewitness back then." Why am I reminding them of that? I think Richard is guilty. I met him up in prison. He's been taking money from Audrey all these years. He's a slime.

"He had blood on his sweatshirt and footprints leading in from the garage and bloody prints on the carpet," countered Jonathan. "My brother did it."

"Of course he had blood on him. He held his wife, tried to see if she was still alive," said Audrey. Her face was red.

"Brooks, you know how I've felt about this all along. What do you want with me?" asked Jonathan.

"You're the best defense lawyer I know," Brooks argued. "We owe it to your brother to revisit the case. What do you have to lose? Either you confirm your hypothesis, or you get a chance to get your brother out of prison and spend some years with him before it's too late. Your mama would have wanted that. Family meant everything to her. She'll never rest in peace. Not until her son gets justice."

"Don't bring my mama into this."

Susan broke into the conversation. "Why did you ask *me* here, Brooks?"

"I know that you and your daughter Lynette…" He paused. "*And* Audrey found the missing glove in the wrong evidence box. I know you've been in contact with Richard."

Jonathan raised his eyebrows.

"So what?" Susan demanded. "You already have a private investigator. Why do you need me?"

"It's Richard who wants you. He told me if I wanted to help build a case, I had to involve Susan Wiles. Not sure why he was so insistent."

Mike, who had been quietly listening and observing the whole time, said, "This is a bad idea. If you want to build a case, put it together yourself. You don't need my wife's help. We're heading home." He paused. "Right after the play-offs game."

Audrey pleaded, "Susan, don't go home. I've seen you in action. You can help clear Richard. I know you can."

"Who says I'm speaking to you?" said Susan. "After how you lied to me?"

Jonathan looked back and forth between the two women. "What does she mean, Audrey?"

Audrey glared at Susan. "Nothing. She doesn't mean anything."

Jonathan said, "Susan, if I were you, I'd get as far away from this situation as possible. Why help a murderer go free? I'm getting out of here." He headed toward the door.

Brooks said, "No, wait! Please. How about we meet with the witness, and if you're both not convinced Richard is innocent after that, you step away. Please. Just do that much."

"You know I'm in," said Audrey. "We owe it to Richard."

How can a woman intelligent enough to have run a school for decades be so easily duped? thought Susan.

"I owe him nothing," said Jonathan.

Like a second-rate actor, Brooks took the stage. "Poor Abigail Stirling. Tossing and turning up there in heaven all these years." He turned his eyes toward the ceiling as he spoke.

"I said to leave my mama out of it."

Wow, that's a tender spot. Jonathan loved his mother—my grandmother! Susan observed.

The room was warm in spite of the open window. Susan felt as though she'd choke without some fresh air.

"He's your brother!" pleaded Brooks. "What if he dies in prison, and then you discover he was innocent? What if the real murderer has been getting away with killing Maggie all these years? Do it for Abigail, if nothing else." *He's been watching too many television evangelists. Listen to that exaggerated passion,* Susan said to herself.

Jonathan moved toward the door.

Brooks grabbed his arm. "And there's something else. Another piece of evidence."

"You're bluffing."

"Stay until after we talk to the witness. Then I'll share the missing piece to this puzzle."

Susan looked at Mike. *Yes, this whole thing sounds fishy.* After all, she disliked Richard and could totally imagine him as a killer. He was a player. He talked Audrey into giving him money and depleting her finances, allowing her to hire attorney after attorney to look into his case. Audrey's son (Susan's half brother) had even reached out to Susan for help getting Audrey to drop the issue after he discovered the amount of debt Audrey had incurred trying to prove Richard's innocence.

"I can count on you, Susan. Right?"

The thought of working with Audrey turned her stomach. And how could she act natural around Jonathan, concealing the fact that she was his daughter? Would she be able to keep up the charade? She wasn't sure she even wanted to try.

"Susan, what do you say?" said Brooks. His body bubbled like a newly-opened bottle of champagne.

Curiosity got the better of her. What missing puzzle piece? Maybe she could help prove Richard *was* guilty once and for all. She looked at Mike, who simply shrugged his shoulders. She turned to Jonathan. "I'll stay if you agree to work on this too. You and I both think Richard Stirling is guilty. Brooks says you're the best defense attorney around, so if you can't prove he's innocent, Audrey and Brooks will drop this forever. Right?" She looked from Audrey to Jonathan.

"Okay," said Jonathan. "I'll dig through the evidence once again, meet with this so-called witness, and put this case to bed once and for all."

"Do we have a deal?" asked Brooks.

Susan shook his hand. "Yes, Brooks. We have a deal."

Chapter 3

The leisurely stroll to the meeting felt like a leg of the Iditarod returning to the hotel. Susan popped two Excedrin into her mouth. Her father, right before her in the flesh—she hadn't been ready for that. He was tall, good-looking, soft-spoken, with that southern accent. Like Audrey, he acted years younger than his biological age. Should she tell him she was his daughter? She wasn't ready for the emotional investment. But didn't he deserve to know? She was still furious at Audrey for not telling her Jonathan Stirling was her father. She plopped down on the bed.

Mike put his arm around her. "Are you okay?"

"What do you think?" Susan's veins bulged just picturing Audrey, and her nerves felt raw after meeting her birth father. "Remember how upset I was when I first found out I was adopted? Jonathan's liable to react the same way."

"That's true, but the longer you wait, the worse it will be. Right now he'd be angry with Audrey. You just found out who he was, but the longer you wait and deliberately keep it from him, the madder he's apt to be at you."

She jumped at the sound of a knock. When Mike opened the door, Susan's face fell when she saw Audrey Roberts standing there. "What are you doing here? Why did you follow us?"

"Susan, you can't tell Jonathan he's your father. Please. If he knows, he'll be too distracted to build Richard's case."

"Are you kidding me? You've lied to me and to my father for sixty-three years. You're facing him after all this time. I may very well tell him the truth, and *that's* what you're worried about? Jonathan being too *distracted* to get your boyfriend out of jail?"

"He has no idea he's your father. He'll be furious if he finds out I kept it from him."

"That's all the *more* reason to tell him. *I'm* furious at you. Does that matter?"

Mike stepped in. "Audrey, you shouldn't have lied to Susan and Jonathan. It's Susan's call as to whether or not she wants to stay, and it's up to her if she wants to tell Jonathan."

Susan was more determined than ever to nail Richard's fate and prove he was guilty, if for no other reason than to make Audrey miserable. Jonathan was supposedly a great lawyer, and *he* believed Richard was guilty. She could live with keeping Audrey's secret long enough to let Jonathan seal Richard's fate. Besides, she needed time to process this new relationship.

"Fine, Audrey. For now."

"Thank you, Susan." Audrey stepped forward to hug Susan, but Susan turned away. "We'll work together on this, but after that, I don't want to see you again." Susan watched Audrey's face and neglected to see any sign of hurt or regret. She knew getting her lover-boy Richard out of jail and keeping peace with Jonathan were Audrey's priorities.

Later that night, Susan's anger made it difficult to sleep. She flipped from her side to her stomach, tried different arrangements of pillows, lowered the thermostat, but her mind couldn't release her anger at Audrey enough to allow her body to relax. In the morning, she was totally committed to confirming Richard's guilt. Jonathan Stirling was a professor emeritus at the Iberton University Law School. After a quick breakfast, Susan and Mike made their way to his office.

Brooks rose from the chair across from Jonathan's roll top desk. "Susan, Mike, I hope you slept well. Have a seat."

They sat on the leather sofa against the paneled wall. Jonathan offered them a cup of coffee.

The door swung open, and a breathless Audrey said, "Where's the witness? Is he here yet? I got here as fast as I could." Audrey looked well rested and pulled a notepad and pen out of her purse. She smiled at Susan, who immediately looked away. Susan caught Jonathan's eye and remembered she had to be careful about showing too much emotion toward either him or Audrey. It wouldn't be a big leap for Jonathan to put together the facts. Susan was Audrey's daughter and just the right age to have been conceived the summer Audrey and Jonathan were together. In fact, Susan wondered just who he assumed Susan's father was.

Jonathan led them to the conference table. Susan took Mike's hand and pulled him to the seat farthest away from Audrey. They were barely settled when there was a knock at the door. Brooks ushered in a forty-something Grizzly Adams look-alike wearing a flannel shirt and Levis.

So this is the witness. He'll look really credible if this case ever sees a courtroom. She imagined him clean-shaven, wearing a suit. Maybe with a little makeover...

Brooks shook his hand and introduced everyone. "We're delighted you came all the way from Maine."

"I still don't know how you found me. I live off the radar. Had it been winter, you'd never have made it up the path to my cabin."

Susan was a bit surprised. Brooks went all the way to Maine to find this character. He must really have a stake in clearing Richard's name.

Jonathan began. "So Mr. Schumaker, why don't you tell us what you saw the night Maggie Stirling was murdered."

"You can call me Axel. I was just a kid, ten years old. I was in my room doing homework when I heard a car backfire. I looked out the window. It was snowing, just some flurries. I saw a green van, one of those VW ones like the hippies used to paint flowers all over in the sixties. It pulled into our neighbor's driveway. The garage and porch lights were on at the Stirling's, otherwise I wouldn't have seen nothing."

"What time was that?" asked Jonathan.

"I don't know exactly. It was after dinner. It was already dark out."

Brooks said, "Did you see anyone get out of the van?"

"Yep, I did. Just saw the back of him mostly until–"

"Until what?" said Brooks.

"When he pulled open the garage door, he turned around, like he was making sure nobody was watchin'."

This guy sounds like a hillbilly. What judge is going to take him seriously? Susan sipped her lukewarm coffee.

"What did he look like?" asked Jonathan.

"He was wearing a hat, one of those knitted snow cap things we all wore. He was white and had glasses. It was pretty far away, but that's what I remember."

"Then what happened? How long was he in their house?"

"I dunno. I went back to doing my homework, then went downstairs to get a snack and watch some TV with my dad."

Susan heard Audrey sigh. She was mesmerized by every word Axel Schumaker uttered, not even pausing to blink.

Brooks continued. "Did your dad hear the van?"

"No, he always drank a few beers and fell asleep in the La-Z-Boy after dinner. He was sleeping when I came into the den."

The wheels were turning inside Susan's head. Didn't this ten-year-old boy think it strange to see a van pull into the neighbor's driveway after dark, then see a stranger open the garage door and go inside? She looked over at Audrey. Look at her sitting on the edge of her seat. Glued to every word this guy is saying.

"So you definitely saw a stranger go into the Stirling's house that night. You didn't see a black Lincoln in the driveway, did you? Richard drove a black Lincoln Town Car."

"Nope. There was a red compact in the driveway. Mrs. Stirling must have gone in through the front door."

Jonathan said, "So you'd be willing to testify that you saw a green van in the Stirling driveway the night Maggie Stirling was murdered?"

"I guess so," said Axel.

Susan found his tone unconvincing. If he was so certain he saw the van that night, he would have tried to convince his parents to vouch for him. Even if he wasn't a credible witness back then, he's had thirty years to come forward. And why is he living like a hermit up in Maine?

Susan said, "Axel, what made you move to Maine?"

"I like the quiet. No one bothers you. I can hunt and fish to my heart's delight. Anything else?"

"Not at the moment. Thanks, we'll be in touch," said Brooks. He led Axel out the door.

"See," said Audrey. "With his testimony, they'll have to let Richard go. How long till they release him?"

Jonathan answered, "There's no guarantee Richard is getting out. Axel Schumaker was ten years old, and all this time has gone by. He can't give a definite time or description of who he saw. It could have been Richard himself sneaking back home in a friend's car. Richard wears glasses. We'll need more."

Audrey stood up. "Wait a minute. Brooks, you said you had new evidence. You said you'd tell us about it after we met the witness."

"That's right," said Susan.

"I checked through Maggie's financial records," replied Brooks.

"And... get to the point," said Jonathan.

"The week she was murdered, Maggie made a large deposit. There were also several previous ones. I'm thinking she could have been blackmailing someone or taking bribes."

"She was a real estate agent. She probably sold a house," said Susan. She makes huge deposits into her bank account, and we find out about it thirty years later?

"If she sold a house, it would go into a business account until the seller claimed it," said Mike.

"Unless she was hiding it from the business," said Susan.

Brooks said, "She worked with another agent. We can track him down later when we go up to New York. If he's still alive and still in the area, that is."

"You think we can find the person who was giving Maggie money?" asked Audrey.

"Possibly. If so, it's reasonable doubt," answered Brooks.

Jonathan shook his head. "It's only reasonable doubt if we can make it sound reasonable. At the moment it's pure conjecture. She could have been selling off collectibles for all we know."

"I have one more possibility," said Brooks. "Jonathan, Audrey, do you remember Maggie's sister? She was a few years older than us."

"I do remember," said Audrey. "Adair. Adair Porter. She was a wild one, that sister of hers. Got into trouble with drugs, stole from her parents. They wound up disowning her or something like that."

Brooks added, "Maggie's the one who turned Adair in to the police for buying drugs. The parents disowned her, cut her out of the will. After they died, she unsuccessfully contested the will. Last I heard she still lives in town. Waits tables, lives in the mobile home park. Not married far as I know."

"Why wasn't she a suspect?" asked Susan.

"She was living here in Atlanta, poor as a church mouse. Never would have had the money to fly up to New York. I suppose that's why she wasn't a suspect, but come to think of it, there was a whole lot of hatred there," said Brooks.

"We have to look into her," said Audrey.

Audrey's desperation is making me sick, Susan thought. She's grasping at straws. Brooks is right there behind her. *Let's get this over with so Mike and I can go tour the Carter Center*. She stood up. "So what's our plan of action?"

"Let's locate Adair Porter and go from there," said Jonathan. "I'll check public records and make sure she's still alive. If so, Brooks, see if you can find out where she is. Susan, Mike, and Audrey, see if you can find any evidence she was in New York at the time of Maggie's murder. We'll meet back here tomorrow morning."

Chapter 4

Mike and Susan left Jonathan's office and walked across the street for an early lunch. Antique streetlights and wrought iron planters lined the sidewalk. They passed an eclectic array of shops and restaurants, choosing to eat at a small sandwich shop. Susan picked up the aroma of split pea soup as soon as they opened the door.

"This place is charming. And I'm sure you can get a heart-healthy turkey sandwich. Look, they have whole-grain baguettes." Susan pointed to the menu behind the take-out counter.

"Great," said Mike. "And they have baked potato chips. At least that will make it more palatable." Mike rolled his eyes at his wife, who had become his personal food warden since his heart attack a few months ago.

"After lunch let's go over to the law library and try to find out what we can about Adair Porter. Surely we can find articles about her family and the inheritance situation. The Porters were society stars back then." Susan took a pad of paper and a pen from her purse. "There are some things I'd like to find out about Richard and Brooks while we're there as well."

After the waitress took their order, Susan started writing. "Brooks, Richard, and Jonathan knew each other since high school."

Mike added, "Maggie and Audrey were in that group too. Didn't they go to some ritzy prep school?"

Susan added it to the list. "That's right. Audrey and Jonathan got together and had me. Jonathan didn't know Audrey was pregnant. He went out of state to law school. After graduation, he came back here to Atlanta and opened a practice."

The food came quickly. Susan blew on a spoonful of soup, then took a bite of her egg salad sandwich. Mike picked up his crunchy turkey baguette, spilling crumbs onto his plate as he dug in.

Mike said, "Richard went into business, married Maggie, and moved to New York State."

"Brooks went to law school right here at Iberton. He said something about Richard giving him a job after he left law school. Why did he leave law school to become a paralegal? *After I was forced to leave law school—* those are the words he used."

"Maybe the stress was making him sick. Who knows?" Mike poured the remnants of the chips into his mouth, tapping the bottom of the bag to get every last crumb. "I'm about done. Why don't we head over to the law library?"

They crossed the street and walked into the library, which looked out of place amidst the surrounding stone buildings.

Mike looked at the glass walls and chrome elevators. "They must have added this later. Successful universities are always expanding."

Susan led Mike past sleek black tables and metal stacks, directly to the reference section. Susan ran her hands over the textured spines. She enlisted the help of the reference librarian, who pulled up information on Adair and the rest of the Porter family. While many libraries had converted their old files into a digital format, this one still had their old newspapers on microfilm. It had been a while since Susan had read microfiche, and she had to position her bifocals in just the right spot.

Mike sat next to her. "Here's an article about a holiday extravaganza at the Porter house. Look, it's the Porters with two smiling daughters—Margaret and Adair. They're beautiful. What a shame that Adair went over to the dark side."

Susan looked over his shoulder. "Looks like a mansion. I'll bet Richard realized the family fortune was quite hefty and set his sights on marrying Maggie."

"Don't jump to conclusions. Here's another article about a debutante ball. Says Maggie went to a prep school called Tarrington Academy. Guess the whole crew did."

Susan jotted down the name of the school and the date of the ball, noting Adair's absence in the family photo. She searched for Tarrington Academy, which she found was still in existence. According to the information, several alumni went on to become famous actors or politicians. She scrolled through. "Jimmy Carter was the keynote speaker at a graduation in the eighties."

"He still lives here as far as I know."

"Look, Mike. There was a terrible fire during the time our brat pack was in attendance. This article says the girls' dorm burned to the ground. One student died in the fire. Arson was suspected but never proven."

"Maggie and Audrey must have lived there too. It's a small school. I doubt there was more than one girls' dorm." Mike found the obituaries for Mr. and Mrs. Porter. "The parents died together in a car crash. Poor girls. Maggie was still at Tarrington, and Adair must have been in her early twenties at the time."

"Want to take a ride to Tarrington?" Susan looked up the address on her phone and discovered it was accessible by train.

Mike said, "I thought you wanted to go to the Carter Center?"

"First things first." They caught MARTA right outside the campus.

"What is it we're hoping to find?" asked Mike.

"Maybe some info on Richard and Maggie's relationship. Was it genuine? Was he abusive? Did Maggie have a longtime enemy who could have followed her to New York and killed her?" Susan shuddered. "Mike, I feel like someone is watching us."

Mike scanned the half-full train car. "I see someone sleeping, and the others are either buried in newspapers or on their laptops. It's your imagination."

"I've been on edge since we got here. I guess you're right."

They exited into the fall sunlight and walked toward the school. *What's that crunching sound? Am I being tailed?* She whipped her head around and thought she caught a glimpse of someone darting around a corner. *Shake it off. Who on earth cares if Mike and I are headed to a prep school.* A few steps later a gated brick building came into view, and they followed the signs leading to the administrative building.

Susan squinted as she and Mike entered. In the dim lighting the plush carpet appeared blood red. A pleasant young receptionist behind an old-fashioned oak desk offered to help them. Susan explained what they needed.

"Mr. Snow has been here that long. So has Mrs. Roth. They're both teaching right now. Elaine Alexander is retired, but she volunteers in the library. She's probably there now," said the receptionist. She pointed them in the direction of the library.

"I hope Elaine Alexander can give us some insights," said Susan. They walked along the brick sidewalk. Susan jumped. "Did you hear that?"

Mike looked around. "You have to calm down. It was just the wind. Hey, this is the building."

In contrast to the modern law library at Iberton, Tarrington's ground floor library was furnished with heavy wooden tables and pub-style chairs. Susan drank in the warm aroma of musty old books and was reminded of the libraries she grew up with. Students worked at the tables and study carrels. The reference desk, manned by a sweet-looking elderly lady, was easily visible.

Susan approached the desk and introduced herself. "We are looking for Elaine Alexander. I was told she volunteers here."

The woman smiled. "She sure does. I'm Elaine Alexander. What can I help you with?"

"I'm sure this sounds odd, but my husband and I are looking for information about students who attended school here some thirty-plus years ago. Their names are Margaret Porter, Audrey Roberts, Brooks Churchill, and two brothers—Richard and Jonathan Stirling." She swallowed hard. "Audrey Roberts is my mother." She almost added the part about Jonathan Stirling being her father but choked on the words.

"Audrey's daughter. My how the years fly. Yes, I remember them. My body's starting to go, but I pride myself on my keen mental faculties. What do you want to know?"

"I'm writing sort of a memoir from my mother's point of view. It's a gift for her birthday." Mike cocked his head at her. "What was my mother like back then? I saw pictures in her yearbook. What were her friends like?"

"Jonathan was one of my favorites—polite, smart. He and Audrey Roberts were an item. The golden couple if you will. Audrey was ambitious, wanted to run her own school one day. The brother, he was a player. Had the girls falling all over him but had no respect for any female on this campus, including his female teachers. Got himself into all sorts of trouble. If it weren't for his parents—big donors to the school—he'd have gotten thrown out his first semester."

"How about Brooks Churchill?"

"The curly blond with the wire glasses—he was an odd sort. Friends with both Jonathan and Richard, even though the two brothers were at opposite poles personality-wise. He had a girlfriend who died right here on campus in that awful fire."

Pretending she hadn't already read about it, Susan said, "What awful fire?"

"The girls' dorm caught fire one Saturday night. Fortunately many of the girls were out at the Homecoming Dance, but a few stayed behind. We lost a dear girl that night. Brooks never fully recovered."

The bell rang to signal the change of classes. Elaine looked at her watch. "It's time for me to go. I only volunteer half days. Anything else I can help you with?"

Mike said, "One last thing. Maggie Porter. What can you tell us about her?"

"Quiet, strait-laced. Didn't say a whole lot. Smart girl. Lost her parents in a car accident her junior year and retreated into her own little shell. Richard moved in on her afterward, and she wound up marrying him. Moved to New York and was murdered in her own home. Richard killed her. We all knew it. He's serving a life sentence if he's even still alive."

"How did Jonathan and Richard get along?"

"Those two were like oil and water—yin and yang, angel and devil… If you didn't know better, you'd never peg them as brothers." Elaine looked again at her watch. "Well, gotta get going or I'll miss my train."

"Thanks for your time. You've been quite helpful."

Susan and Mike headed out of the building. The few students remaining on the sidewalk hustled inside to their classes when a second bell rang. Susan was satisfied with the information she'd learned. Elaine had confirmed her feelings about Richard. He was a snake, just as she'd suspected, and she wasn't at all convinced of his innocence. It was nice to hear that her biological father was polite and likeable. In the short time she'd been around him, she'd formed the same impression. He reminded her of the dad she grew up with—the only father she'd known until recently.

Walking back to the train, Susan felt the hair on the back of her neck prickle. She whispered to Mike. "Slow down, and when I say go, turn around and see if you see anyone. Humor me."

Susan slowed the pace and listened for footsteps against the sidewalk.

"Why are we doing this?"

"You'll see."

She grabbed Mike's hand and said *now*. They whipped around and Susan screamed. They were face to face with Audrey.

Chapter 5

Audrey screamed, "Are you trying to give me a heart attack?"

"What are you doing here?" said Susan. "Are you following us?" She turned to Mike. "She's following us!" She felt her face heating up.

"I wasn't... I mean I was... but I'm the one who should be upset here." Her tone changed from tentative to angry. "Why did you go to Tarrington without me? Brooks said we were supposed to work together and find out about Adair Porter. Why were you and Mike sneaking around, digging up information on us?"

Mike said, "It was a whim. Susan thought we might find out if Maggie had any enemies from her student days. We're waiting for Brooks to confirm Adair is alive before we go about looking for thirty-year-old tickets to New York."

"You could have included me," said Audrey. She folded her arms tightly over her chest.

Susan couldn't hold back. "I don't even want to be in the same room with you, let alone work together. You dragged me into this case. I don't have to help you, you know. We can get on the next plane back to New York."

"Now, ladies," said Mike, stepping in between them. "The sooner we get the information we need, the sooner we can all go home. I miss Annalise. Don't you miss our grandbaby, Susan?"

She hated when Mike played on her vulnerabilities. "Okay. We'll work together if it helps solve this sooner."

Susan's phone vibrated. "Yes, Brooks. Really? How about if the three of us go out to the trailer park, and you check out the diner?"

"I take it Brooks found out she's still alive," said Mike.

"And he has an address for her. He's texting it to me now."

"What are we waiting for? Let's go," said Audrey. Susan rolled her eyes.

The taxi ride took them past the suburban area near the school. Soon they saw farmhouses, empty lots, and a sign for Miller's Trailer Park. Susan could have sworn she heard a cow mooing.

"There it is," said Susan. "I've seen some beautiful mobile home parks, but clearly this isn't one of them." They walked through broken glass, inhaling the smell of rotten garbage as they worked their way to the rental office located in a double-wide trailer. A crooked sign in the window read *vacansies,* with an *s* in place of the *c.* "Illiterates. How do people live like this?"

"Makes you thankful for what you have," said Audrey. "Adair grew up surrounded by nice things. Must have been hard for her."

"Can I help you?" A middle-aged woman in a stained housecoat stood up from behind a cluttered desk. Susan smelled stale cigarette smoke.

"We're looking for Adair Porter. We were told we could find her here."

"Adair Porter. Name doesn't sound familiar. Got a picture or somethin'?"

Having a hunch it might come in handy, Susan had taken a photo of the newspaper clipping she'd found at the library. "Here you go. It's old. She's in her fifties now."

"Hmmm. Don't think I know her. Let me ask Pa if he remembers her." She yelled into the kitchen area. "Pa, can you come out here?"

A bald gentleman with several missing teeth and a big gut emerged from the next room. His daughter said, "Do you know this lady? She's a lot older now. Name's Adair Porter."

"Addie Porter. Yes, she lived here for a while. Pretty young thing. Waited tables at the diner down the road. She came into some money and up and left. Good for her."

Mike said, "Do you know where she went?"

"She said she was gonna do some travelin,' then settle down in town. That's the last I heard."

"Did she say where she was traveling to? Ever have visitors, mention family? Boyfriend?"

"Not that I remember. Wait. Said something about having to buy a heavy coat. Guess she was heading north."

Audrey said, "Do you know what diner she worked at?"

"There's only one diner around here. Down the road about a mile."

"Thanks," said Susan. She was thankful they'd asked the cab to wait for them. *Would never have flagged one down here in the middle of Cowville.* She handed the directions to the driver, and they slipped into the backseat.

"I hope we find Adair or someone who can tell us where she is," said Audrey.

Mike said, "It's been a long time. Don't be disappointed if this is a dead end."

Soon they arrived at the diner. Susan was first to spot the bullet-shaped, silver metal trailer. A few older model cars and a motorcycle were parked in front of it.

"Looks like a classic diner to me," said Mike.

"Antiquated is more like it," said Susan. The taxi pulled onto the gravel, and they crawled out into the crisp air.

"It's beautiful up here," said Audrey.

The clanging of pots and pans and the chugging of the dishwasher made their entrance into the diner unnoticeable. Two waitresses were busy wiping tables and filling condiment containers. Another was mopping the floor. It was late for lunch and way too early for dinner, so except for the staff, the diner was empty. Susan eyed the mile-high peach pie and ginormous cookies in the glass case by the cashier. Her stomach growled. *It's always the right time for dessert.*

"Excuse me," said Susan. The waitress stopped mopping.

"Table for three? Booth or counter?"

"Um, booth." They followed the menu-toting waitress to a booth near the window. Susan continued. "We're looking for someone who once worked here. It was many years ago." Susan fumbled in her purse for the photo she'd brought. "Here's a picture."

"I've only been here a few years. Try Betty. She's filling the saltshakers over there. Watch out, the floor's still damp."

Betty was older than the first waitress, and Susan was optimistic she'd remember Adair. Betty studied the picture.

"No, sorry. I don't remember her. Tell you what. Shift changes in about ten minutes. Tammy comes in then. She's been here forever."

"Great," said Mike. "Meanwhile, how about we grab a cup of coffee and some pie while we wait?" Susan shot him the *are you really going to eat a slice of artery clog?* look, but in spite of it, he was the first to ask for peach pie. A la mode, no less. *Not that I haven't been salivating since we walked in,* Susan thought. Betty took their order and returned promptly with three slabs of pie.

"Adair came into money. That's news," said Susan.

"I wonder if she snuck on up to New York and killed Maggie."

"Audrey, she bought the coat before she went traveling. That's what Pa said."

"He never said she went to New York, just that she needed a coat. Hmm, I suppose she could've gone to New York, fought with Maggie, then came back and announced her plans to travel."

Mike put down his fork for the first time since Betty brought over the pie. "We're assuming she had the money to buy a ticket to New York."

The bell over the door rang, signaling a new customer. "Brooks!" said Susan.

Brooks made his way over to the table. "I told you *I'd* check out the diner. Did you find anything at the trailer park? Is she still there? There isn't a death certificate on file. I was hoping she still worked here." Brooks squeezed into the booth next to Audrey.

"She moved out of the trailer park years ago. Apparently came into money. We're waiting for a waitress named Tammy. Tammy's worked here a long time and might remember her."

"I'll bet that's her coming in now," said Audrey.

A pasty-skinned waitress in a pink apron made her way over. "I'm Tammy. Betty says you want to talk to me."

Susan and Audrey explained they were looking for Adair. Tammy shook her head.

"She did work here, but it's been a long time. She was a good girl, that Addie. Responsible, hard worker. We missed her when she left."

"Do you know where she was headed?" asked Brooks.

"As far as I know, she was looking for a place in the city. Was planning on going to school. Nursing, I think she said."

"Thanks, maybe we'll check there." *I love looking for needles in haystacks,* Susan added to herself.

"I wonder if she ever married that boyfriend of hers," said the waitress.

Four pairs of eyes stared at her. "Boyfriend?" said Susan.

"Yeah. A Yankee. Could hardly understand him. He talked so fast like the place was on fire or somethin.'"

Brooks asked, "What was his name?"

"Weird name. Tate, Case, Blake... Chase. That was it. Chase. He was from New York. Don't remember his last name. Worked in construction. Something about being in town to do a project."

"What did he mean by that?" said Audrey.

"You know, a construction project. I figured he was here working on the mall that went up over on Church Street."

Brooks said, "Did Adair ever travel up to New York with him as far as you know?"

"She did. Went up there for Christmas one year. Met his parents. Things were getting serious, then Adair left. I don't know what happened with them after that."

"Thank you," said Brooks. He handed her a card. "Give me a call if you remember anything else."

Chapter 6

Mike worked in the permits office at City Hall back home in Westbrook. The next morning he suggested checking the local building permits for the mall. Knowing the name of the construction company might ultimately lead them to Adair's boyfriend, Chase.

Susan pulled her sweater tightly around her. The air was chillier than she'd expected. Based on the estimate from the concierge, rush hour traffic nearly doubled the time it took the taxi to arrive at City Hall. It let them off in front of a modern, three-story building. Once inside, Mike introduced Susan and himself to the man behind the front counter.

"I'm Mike Wiles. I work in the permits office up in Westbrook, New York. Can we have a look at the permits for the Simmons Mall that went up on Church Street back in 1985?"

"Simmons Mall. Those were filed by hand back then. They're sitting in storage. If you fill out a request form, we can get them in twenty-four to forty-eight hours."

"That would be great," said Mike. Susan made an involuntary *tsk* sound. It was embarrassingly loud, causing both men to look at her. Mike filled out the form.

Once outside, Susan said, "I'm disappointed. I was hoping we could start on this today."

"It's not like they have nothing better to do than hunt up thirty-year-old records. We'll have them soon."

"How about we drop by Jonathan's office? Let's see if he found a record of Adair traveling to New York around the time of the murder." Susan continued, "I never asked what kind of business Richard was involved in. I'm sure Jonathan can answer that. It's possible Maggie's death was related to his work if not her own."

Jonathan was grading papers at his desk when Susan and Mike arrived.

"Susan and Mike. Come on in. Any news?"

"We found out Maggie had a sister named Adair who had problems and was disinherited by her parents. We know she had a boyfriend from New York named Chase something or other who was down here working on the construction of Simmons Mall. She had traveled to New York with him, and we're trying to see if it coincides with time of Maggie's murder. If Maggie inherited the family fortune, Adair may have felt entitled to a share of it."

Jonathan said, "I knew about Adair being cut out of the will, but it was years before Maggie's murder. And why wouldn't she have gone after Maggie here in Atlanta? I doubt Adair was in any shape to plot a murder, go up to New York, and carry it out. She was in and out of rehab or jail ever since I met Maggie. Besides, Maggie sunk most of that money into Richard's construction business. There wouldn't have been much of a fortune to get."

"Construction business?"

"Richard and his friend Carl Black started a construction company here in Atlanta. My idiot of a brother started stealing from the company. Carl found out and was going to prosecute." replied Jonathan.

"Why didn't he?" asked Mike.

"Just about that time, Maggie turned twenty-one and gained control over her trust fund. She paid Carl back every cent, then helped Richard start a new company in New York. By the time she did all that, the trust fund was nearly gone," said Jonathan.

"Why would she sink all her money into a new business? And out of state, no less?" asked Susan.

"Maggie had a real estate license. She figured Richard could build the houses, and she'd sell them. IBM and Ford opened up plants a few months apart, and houses popped up like dandelions," reasoned Jonathan.

"If Maggie had success in her new business, Adair may have followed her," Susan suggested.

"You're grasping at straws." Jonathan shook his head.

"Good," said Susan. "If we can rule out Adair, that's one less suspect you can use as reasonable doubt. We're on the same side here."

Mike asked, "Was the construction business in New York successful?"

"For a while, then Richard screwed up like always and nearly went bankrupt. Maggie filed for divorce and demanded he sell what was left of the company and give her half the profits. We don't have to look any further. Richard had means and motive."

"How did Brooks figure into this?" asked Mike.

"Brooks was kicked out of law school. He says it was his choice, but I know better. Richard hired him as a paralegal to help out with building contracts. Maggie used him for her real estate business as well."

The door creaked open, and Brooks walked into the office.

"Did I hear my name?"

"Speak of the devil," said Jonathan.

"I wanted to come by and tell you I got a lead on finding Adair Porter. I traced her nursing license. She works in a hospital right here in the city."

"Susan said, "That's great. Let's go talk to her.""

Audrey burst through the doorway. "Leaving me out again? I didn't know we had a meeting scheduled." She slammed her purse down on Jonathan's desk.

"Relax," said Jonathan. "It wasn't a scheduled meeting. Susan and Mike dropped by, and Brooks just now came."

"What about Adair? I heard you say something about Adair," said Audrey.

Brooks filled her in. "I found out she's still in Atlanta. She's a nurse."

"Well, let's go talk to her," said Audrey. "I'm sure she did it. She went up to New York and murdered her sister because her parents cut her out of the will." Audrey was half out of the door when Jonathan stopped her.

Jonathan said, "We can't all accost her at work. I'll give her a call and make an appointment."

"We're all included in the meeting, right?"

"Yes, Audrey. No one is trying to keep you in the dark."

Brooks said, "Look, I'll take care of meeting with Adair."

"Then what should we do?" asked Audrey.

Brooks scratched his chin. "You know, I thought of someone else who might be a suspect."

"Who's that?" said Jonathan.

"Remember Carl Black, Richard's business partner here in Atlanta?" said Brooks.

"Yes, but you said Maggie paid him back all the money Richard stole," said Audrey.

"Not before Richard was forced to declare bankruptcy and sell the family home," replied Brooks.

Jonathan said, "I can't see Carl following Richard up to New York and murdering Maggie. *She's* the one who paid him back. Use your common sense, Brooks."

"I wasn't suggesting Carl did it," said Brooks. "He had a wacko son, remember? He threatened to get revenge on Richard, right on camera. Said it to a reporter on the evening news."

"You just now thought of this?" asked Susan.

"We're exploring all possibilities, right?" said Brooks. "I won't let Richard die in prison after all he did for me. *I'll* follow up on Adair Porter, ya'll can follow up on Carl's son. His name was Jake. Jake Black. I'm surprised I remember it."

Chapter 7

After Brooks left, Susan, Mike, Audrey, and Jonathan set out to find information about Jake Black, the son of Richard's former construction partner.

"I only have the one computer in here," said Jonathan. "Two of you should go on over to the law library. It'll be twice as fast."

Susan didn't want to work alone with Audrey, and sensing Audrey's awkwardness around Jonathan, she made a suggestion. "How about I'll stay here with Jonathan, and Mike goes to the library with Audrey."

"Will do," said Mike. "The Braves' game is tonight, so we can't be at this all day." He held the door open for Audrey. "Ladies first. See you back here in two hours."

"We'll put in a few hours, then call it quits. I have a backlog of grading to catch up on anyway."

Susan pulled up a chair next to Jonathan. Sitting so close to her biological father gave her goose bumps. Jonathan googled Jake Black.

"There are hundreds of Jake Blacks in the greater Atlanta area. And we don't know he hasn't left the area in the past thirty years." Jonathan put on his reading glasses.

"If we can't find him, that's one less suspect for reasonable doubt," said Susan.

"Jake Black senior, Jake Black junior..."

"Jonathan, were you ever married?"

"I was married for more than half my life. To the same woman, I might add. I was widowed half a dozen years ago." He continued typing as they spoke.

"I'm sorry. Mike had a heart attack not too long ago. Just the possibility of losing him... I can't imagine how you coped."

"It was hard. Still is. I picked up a few more classes here at the university to keep busy. I was planning on retiring, but now it seems pointless. I'd rather be here than alone at home."

Susan tried her best not to tear up and to keep her voice steady. "Do you have children?"

"Nope. We wanted them. Badly. Never had any luck. It's one of my deepest regrets in life."

I have to keep what I want to say to myself, she thought. *It's taking everything I have not to hug him and tell him he has a daughter.*

"I heard you mention having a daughter."

"Lynette. She's a detective. We also have a son, Evan. He's in medical school."

"You must be proud. Family is important. Richard and I never got along. Since our parents died, it's just me." Jonathan printed pages of Jake Blacks from the computer. "We can call each of these, or try to cross-reference each name with birth records first. It will take some work up front but will save us time in the end."

"Let's go with birth records."

Susan and Jonathan took the list and slowly crossed out names. *This is going to take days. Jonathan has so much patience. I'm already getting bored with this. He has my hands, and he smiles like Lynette.*

They'd only covered half a page by the time Audrey and Mike returned. Audrey's eyes drooped. Mike fidgeted near the door.

"We'd better get going," said Susan. She knew Mike was anxious to get back. "I'll call you in the morning."

In the hotel, Susan stretched out on the bed next to Mike and set the alarm to be sure they wouldn't be late for the game. She suggested going to dinner first, but Mike had his heart set on eating hot dogs at Turner Stadium. *Pick your battles. It's one day. I'll get him back on track tomorrow.*

The stadium was surprisingly full for a weeknight, with a carnival-like atmosphere at the entrance. For a moment Susan had forgotten it was the play-offs. *Tickets to the play-offs. Kudos to me.* She had lucked into buying excellent seats.

Beer, cotton candy, peanuts, ice cream… She and Mike spent a small fortune on concessions while enjoying a close game. The night was cool, and stars filled the Atlanta sky. She hated sports as a rule but tonight found herself caught up in the excitement of the game. During the seventh-inning stretch, her eyes wandered to the billboard ads filling the stadium. Her heart raced. *Jake Black Construction. No way. Right there on a banner before my eyes.* She jotted down the phone number.

"What are you doing?" asked Mike.

"You're not going to believe it." She pointed to the banner. "Jake Black Construction. I'll bet that's our Jake Black."

"Come on. The chances of it being the Jake Black we want are slim, you have to admit."

Susan sighed. "I know. But slim is better than none. It'll take five minutes to try the number tomorrow."

The inning began with a home run. The crowd stood and cheered. *Tomorrow. Tonight I'm going to enjoy this experience with the man I love*, she vowed.

Chapter 8

The next morning, Brooks, Audrey, Susan, and Mike gathered in Jonathan's office. Brooks looked like the cat who'd swallowed the canary. *I wonder if he met with Adair*, thought Susan. *Audrey makes me sick, trying to free that slime ball Richard. I guess it could be worse. At least she didn't marry him while he was in prison. I've heard about women doing that.*

Brooks said, "I met with Adair yesterday. Found her at the hospital."

"Well?" said Audrey. "Wait. I know exactly what you're going to say. She was in New York with her boyfriend and killed her sister when she found out Maggie's real estate business was in the black. I knew it." She slapped her thigh emphasizing the word *knew*.

"Not so fast," said Brooks. "I'm afraid it was a dead end. Her boyfriend at the time was from New York but lived nowhere near where Maggie, Richard, and I lived. She was clear on the other side of the state when Maggie was killed."

Audrey's head dropped down. Susan spotted a few tears on her cheeks. "Maybe he moved and you found the old address."

Shaking his head, Jonathan said, "Did you verify that, Brooks?"

"Of course. I'm afraid that only leaves us with Jake Black and our eyewitness. Any progress finding Jake Black?"

Jonathan started to answer, but Susan broke in. "We may have a lead. At the Braves' game last night, I spotted an advertisement for Jake Black Construction. Giving them a call should be our first order of business."

"And what about Axel, the eyewitness?" said Audrey.

"He's still in town. Jonathan, did you set up a deposition? He's anxious to get back to Maine."

"Yes, Brooks. Tomorrow afternoon. He knows he'll be called to testify if this case goes to trial, right? Did you explain that to him?"

"He's ready and willing."

Jonathan took out the list of Jake Blacks and divvied it up amongst them. He handed a page to Audrey and another to Brooks. He was about to hand a page to Susan when she said, "Do you mind if Mike and I catch a cab over to Jake Black Construction?"

Mike said, "We have no idea if that's the Jake Black we want. That's crazy."

Jonathan said, "Maybe it's worth going over there in person. If he *is* the one we're looking for, he might be skeptical about admitting it over the phone."

Mike shrugged his shoulders. Jonathan pulled up the company on his computer and jotted down the address on a small sticky note and handed it to Susan.

After a short cab ride, Mike and Susan arrived at Jake Black Construction just before lunchtime. Smokestacks topped the roofs, and the entrance was next to a big green dumpster. The putrid smell of rotten food made Susan feel like she was about to toss her cookies. She was glad it was daytime and Mike was with her. *This feels like a murder scene straight out of* Law and Order.

Mike said, "You've thought this through, right? Do you know what you're going to say to him? How about, 'My husband and I saw an advertisement for your company at Turner Stadium and because your father was partners with Richard Stirling, the one who stole from the company and caused your Dad to declare bankruptcy, we figured you traveled to New York and killed Richard Stirling's wife. Of course, Stirling's wife's the one who returned the money to your father, but that's beside the point.' That what you had in mind?"

"Well, when you say it like that… It's all in the presentation. I'll be subtle." She led him to the door. They introduced themselves to the receptionist and were told to have a seat in the waiting area. While they were waiting, Mike received a call.

"It was the permits office. They have the information we requested. After this, let's swing by and pick it up."

They waited for nearly an hour on a worn-out gray sofa, flipping through old issues of business magazines. Susan was soon bored and watched the receptionist instead. She had two stacks of files on her desk, some green, some manila. She sorted them as she went through the stack. She put the green ones in the filing cabinet as expected. The manila ones she locked in a cabinet built into the bookcase.

Susan's legs needed stretching, so she got up and went to the water cooler, which happened to take her past the receptionist's desk where a few folders remained. Glancing sideways as she walked, she noticed the labels. The green ones were labeled with what looked like project names, such as Windmere Hotel, and Faraday School. The manila ones had the same labels but were sealed with clear tape and marked *Private*. She sat back down and waited another half an hour before being ushered into Jake Black's office.

Contrary to the bravado she'd feigned when discussing this with Mike, Susan's knees shook uncontrollably. She held onto Mike's arm.

Jake Black was in his late thirties or early forties. His hair was tinged with gray, and Susan was struck by his statuesque height. He wore a wrinkle-free dress shirt and a conservative blue tie.

"What can I help you with?"

"I'm Susan Wiles, and this is my husband, Mike. I'm warning you this is going to sound strange. I'm doing my mother a favor. Her friend, Richard Stirling, is in jail for murdering his wife. After thirty years, new evidence has come to light, which may result in Mr. Stirling getting a new trial. We know he had a business partner named Carl Black, and we are looking for his son. By any chance are you Carl Black's son?" She held her breath, waiting for him to confirm or deny that he was Carl Black's son.

"Yes, I'm Carl Black's son. My dad died several years ago, and I took over the company. What do you want from me?"

"We're looking for information. I hate to ask you this, but we heard that you threatened to kill Richard Stirling on camera because he caused your family to go bankrupt and lose your home all those years ago."

"I'm embarrassed to admit it's true. I was a young hothead back then. Don't get me wrong, I was super angry. Took a long time to let go of that hatred. I said it, but lots of people say things they don't mean when they're angry. If I had a dime for every time I heard the phrase, 'I'll kill you,' I'd be even richer than I am." He chuckled briefly. "Why would I have gone after Richard's wife? If anything, I'd have gone after him."

Susan explained, "I know it's crazy, but anything you can tell us. . . . We're just exploring possibilities."

"It all worked out. My Dad rebuilt the company stronger than ever after Stirling's wife returned the stolen money. I certainly had no reason to kill Maggie Stirling."

"Thanks for your time," said Susan. She and Mike left the office and hailed a taxi.

"Let's run over to the permits office," said Mike. "I know Brooks already crossed Adair off the suspect list, but since I requested the mall permits, I at least have to pick them up."

After picking up the information, Susan and Mike sat on a bench outside City Hall and perused the documents.

"Look, Mike. Black Construction built Simmons Mall. That means the company hired Chase. I'll bet Jake Black can access personnel records and give us Chase's last name."

"What's the point? Chase's family lived clear on the other side of the state from the Stirlings. Brooks already told us that."

"I know. I just have a feeling it may be important. I can't put my finger on it."

"Fine. We're not far, so let's get it over with."

When they returned to Jake Black Construction, the receptionist's chair was empty. "She's probably at lunch," said Susan. "Come on." She led Mike down the hall to Jake Black's office. The door was ajar, and Susan heard Jake yelling at someone over the phone.

"How did this get out?" said Jake. "Thirty years later? Bury it. Now. And if anyone gets in the way, you know what to do." He slammed the phone back onto the cradle.

Susan whispered to Mike, "Let's get out of here before he sees us." They tiptoed away from Jake Black's office. "Something tells me Jake Black isn't someone we want to cross."

Chapter 9

Susan and Mike scurried down the hall. Susan heard the office door fly open as if someone pushed it hard. "Let's go." Then she heard footsteps coming closer by the minute. "Hurry, Mike." They scooted around a corner and down another hallway. It was lunchtime, and the halls were empty.

"Look, over there," said Mike. He pointed to a door at the end of the hallway with a red exit sign above it.

"Mike, this isn't the way we came in."

"We can't turn around now." When they reached the door, Susan grabbed the handle.

"Wait! Don't pull it," said Mike. "It's an emergency exit. The alarm will go off."

"What now?" Susan heard the crescendo of Jake Black's footsteps as they came closer and closer to the bend in the corridor. "Mike, he's going to see us in a second."

"Come on; in here." Mike pulled her into the men's bathroom.

"What if he opens the door?"

"Come on," said Mike. "Stand up on the toilet and close the stall door. I'll be in the next one."

Susan felt her pants tear as she stepped up onto the toilet seat. Twice she lost her balance and nearly fell in. She froze. *Someone is opening the door.* She held her breath and concentrated on staying completely still. *Please, God. Don't let him check the stalls.* She heard him open the first stall door. *I'm going to die. This can't be good for Mike's heart condition.* The second door opened. *Oh, God. Mine's next.* Sweat dripped down her face. Then...

Jake's phone rang at just the right moment. "What? Are you kidding me? Get the team together. This is a financial emergency. I'll be right there." Susan heard Jake stomp out of the bathroom. Whatever the emergency was, it took priority over finding out who was eavesdropping. She still didn't dare move.

"Come on, let's get out of here," said Mike. He helped her down from the toilet. "That was close."

"He's hiding something," said Susan.

"Maybe so, but we can't let him know we suspect him. He doesn't know it was us he was following. As far as he knows, we'd already left some time ago."

"Let's get back to Jonathan's office and fill him in. Looks like Jake Black is our prime suspect."

"He's our only suspect," said Mike.

"What about the personnel records? Don't we still want Chase's last name?"

"Brooks has already eliminated Adair, so I don't see why."

"Just a hunch. Chase worked for Carl Black; he went out with Adair. It might be important somehow. Maybe he can tell us more about Jake Black if nothing else. Let's stop at Human Resources."

"Are you crazy? What if Jake decides to go to lunch and sees us still in the building? Besides, what makes you think Human Resources is going to share that information with us?"

"I have an idea." Susan dragged Mike down the hall to Human Resources. She pulled out her phone and took a picture of the office door.

"What are you doing?" said Mike.

"Finding out Chase's last name. Come on. Let's get back to the university."

Chapter 10

Brooks, Audrey, and Jonathan were gathered at the conference table still sorting through lists of Jake Blacks when Susan and Mike arrived.

"We found the correct Jake Black," said Susan out of breath. "We had a bit of a close call."

Audrey jumped up. "What kind of close call?"

"The man we spoke to admitted he was the Jake Black who made the threat against Richard live on the evening news. He convinced us it was an empty threat made by an angry kid. But then..."

"Then what?" said Audrey. She appeared to hang on to Susan's every word, encouraging an especially lively recount.

"We left and came back. When we returned, we heard Jake on the phone. He told someone to 'bury this.' We assumed he meant when he said he was going to kill Richard Stirling, live on TV."

Mike continued, "We walked away, but Jake must have heard us. He followed us down the hall. We ducked into the men's room..."

"Then we stood on the toilets, and he started opening the stalls."

Audrey's eyes opened wide. "Are you serious? Did he find you?"

"No," said Susan. "Just as he was about to open the door..." She paused and looked straight at Audrey. "His phone rang, and he went back to his office."

"Just like that?" said Audrey.

Jonathan grabbed Susan's hands. She couldn't help noticing how his long fingers resembled her own. "Are you okay?"

"We're fine, but we have to follow up on Jake Black."

Brooks offered to do some footwork and see what he could find out. He grabbed a legal pad and jotted down bits of what Susan had said about their encounter.

"Brooks, did you ever find out Chase's last name?" said Susan.

"No, I didn't pursue it after talking to Adair. Didn't see the point." He walked to the door. "I'm going to get started on this. I'll see you tomorrow after Axel Schumaker's deposition."

"I'll come with you," said Audrey.

After they left, Susan asked Jonathan where she could get an employment application for the university.

Jonathan looked puzzled. "They're online. Why?"

"I had an idea about finding out Chase's last name. Is there some kind of employment verification form?"

Jonathan went to the employment site. "It's right here. I'll print you a copy. What are you planning?"

Susan took the sheet off the printer and grabbed a pen while Mike and Jonathan stood over her shoulder. "See."

Mike said, "It says Chase, but the last name is illegible."

"Exactly," said Susan. "It's all part of the plan. Do you have an envelope, Jonathan?"

She took the envelope, turned to the photos on her phone, and wrote an address. "Do you have a stamp?"

Jonathan fished a stamp out of his desk drawer. "This is going to give us Chase's last name? How?"

"You'll see. Come on, Mike. We'll drop it in the mailbox on the way back to the hotel."

The first thing Susan did back at the hotel was to change out of her torn pants. It was midafternoon but seemed much later given all the excitement they'd had. She turned the TV on softly and stretched out on the bed. She dozed off, but was jarred awake by the sound of her phone. She didn't recognize the number, but given she'd only given contact information to a handful of key people here in Atlanta, she answered it.

"Hello. Yes, this is Susan Wiles. Mr. Snow? From Tarrington Academy. That's right, my husband and I spoke to Elaine Alexander. She did? Sure, where should we meet?" Susan grabbed the notepad and pen from the nightstand. "We'll see you in an hour."

"What was that about?" said Mike.

"It was Mr. Snow. Remember the receptionist at Tarrington said he was one of the faculty members who worked back when the brat pack was there."

"How did he get your number?"

"I gave it to Elaine Alexander. She told him we're looking into Richard Stirling and company. He says he has something important to tell us, so we're meeting him at Starbucks in an hour."

Chapter 11

Susan loved nothing better than the aroma of fresh ground coffee that greeted them at the door. She ordered a pumpkin latte, excited it was back on the menu for fall. Mike ordered a plain black coffee and added a touch of skim milk. *Look at all those table hoggers camped out with their laptops. I hope we can find a place to sit.* They wandered through the shop. *Here's a table by the window.* She sat across from Mike.

"I like Jonathan more and more. He's kind and patient. You know, he told me he regretted never having kids of his own. He was married for a long time."

"Are you considering telling him you're his daughter?"

"I go back and forth. It would be a huge emotional scene for both of us. Maybe after we finish working on the case. I feel a little like I did with Audrey. I grew up with a father and a mother. It feels wrong for Jonathan to take Dad's place."

"You already went through that when you found Audrey. She and Jonathan are your birth parents. Period. The parents you grew up with and loved will always be your real parents. You can consider Jonathan more of a friend, like you did Audrey."

"Audrey's not a friend."

"I said did. Past tense. You're mad at her now, but in any case, you never thought of her the way you think of your mom."

Susan got up and ordered coffee refills. She fidgeted and checked her watch every few minutes. Mr. Snow was almost half an hour late. Mike drummed his fingers on the table and watched out the window.

"Susan, I think he's a no-show. Let's leave."

"We'll give him five more minutes." She resisted the impulse to order a caramel brownie.

Mike stared at the door. "Hey, maybe that's him."

An elderly gentleman wearing a trench coat and tam scanned the room as he joined the coffee line. Susan's eyes met his, and he came over to the table. "I'm Mr. Snow. Are you by any chance Susan and Mike Wiles?"

"Yes, that's us," said Mike.

"I'm sorry I'm late. Traffic was horrendous and parking even worse." He sat at the table and removed his hat.

"You said you wanted to tell us something important." Susan leaned forward across the table.

"Elaine Alexander told me you'd been by asking questions about a group of past students. She said you were looking for information to surprise your mother, but I happen to think that isn't true. I read that Richard Stirling may be getting a new trial."

"Yes. Richard's friend Brooks asked us to help gather evidence. You knew both of them, right?"

"Yes, yes, Mrs. Wiles. I wanted to tell you about Richard. When we at Tarrington heard he'd been arrested for killing his wife all those years ago, none of us were surprised."

"What do you mean?" said Mike.

"Richard had an evil side. Several female students reported being threatened by him during the time he attended our school. One girl said he attacked her. Had a bruise on her cheek to show for it. She teaches at our school now that she's all grown up."

"Really? Do you think she'd mind speaking to us?" Susan gripped the edge of the table.

"I'm sure she wouldn't. She's as sweet now as she was back then. Her students love her. She lives on campus. Oversees the girls' dorm. I'll send her a text letting her know you may be contacting her."

"So you have no doubt Richard killed Maggie?"

"No, ma'am. None at all. In fact, I think he had something to do with Nina Johnson's death too. She's the girl who died in the dorm fire."

Mike said, "What makes you think that?"

"I chaperoned the homecoming dance that night. Richard argued with Nina—made quite a scene. His buddy Brooks stepped in, calmed him down, and left with him. Nina ran out crying shortly afterward."

"We heard Nina had stayed in that night," said Susan.

"Not true. And I'm sure it was arson. A bottle of lighter fluid was found near the dorm. The school kept it out of the papers. It's not the only time Richard was in the area during a suspicious fire either. If you go over to Iberton University, notice the law library. It's much newer than all the surrounding buildings. That's because the original library burned down. Arson was suspected then too. And guess whose construction company was hired to rebuild it."

In unison Susan and Mike answered, "Richard's."

"Richard and his partner, Carl Black. Made a tidy sum on that project, you can bet." Mr. Snow glanced at his watch. "I need to get home and let the dog out. I hope Richard Stirling stays in jail where he belongs. He's a dangerous man."

"Thanks, Mr. Snow. We really appreciate the information." Susan and Mike stood up and shook his hand. After he left, they discussed what they'd just learned.

"Guilty as sin. Just as I thought," said Susan.

"Just as you hoped," said Mike. "Let's get going. I'm starving. Why don't we stop for dinner on the way back? We passed a cute little Mexican place not far from here."

"I'm hungry too. But can we make one stop first?"

"I knew you were going to say that."

Susan's phone rang. She fished it out of her purse and answered.

"Yes, Jonathan. Oh, I was afraid of that. It was a long shot. We'll have to think of another way. We met with Mr. Snow from Tarrington. Lots to tell you. We'll talk soon."

Mike said, "What did Jonathan want?"

"The employee verification form was returned to the university. Jonathan was the contact person. They said the last name was illegible and the date too long ago. They couldn't verify employment for Chase."

"What did you think would happen?"

"It was a long shot. Back to the drawing board. Come on, let's stop by Tarrington Academy before dinner."

Rush hour traffic slowed their journey, but before long they were standing at the front desk in the girl's dorm where a student sorted mail and manned the sign-in sheet.

"Hi, we came to see Elizabeth Wood. Mr. Snow said she lived here."

"Sure. Her apartment is on the top floor. Stairs are around the corner."

Susan and Mike hiked up the steps and knocked on the apartment door. Elizabeth Wood invited them inside. Had they not entered through the dorm, they would think they were in any one of the many apartment complexes interspersed throughout the city. The apartment was tastefully decorated with framed

Picasso and Monet prints on the living room walls. The furnishings were Ikea-style, only sturdier and more expensive-looking.

"Have a seat. Can I get you something to drink? I've got sweet tea, Mr. Pibb, or cold water."

"No thanks," said Susan. "We're on our way to dinner. Mr. Snow mentioned that Richard Stirling attacked you back when you were students."

"Sure did. Mr. Snow said he may be getting out of jail. That would be a terrible mistake."

Mike said, "Did you report it to the police?"

"No, it wouldn't have done any good. I know another of his victims who tried that. The school was desperate to keep it quiet and convinced her not to press charges. She transferred after that."

"Were all the girls afraid of him?" asked Susan.

"Not all. The sensible ones stayed away from him, but he had an eerie charm about him. He dated Nina Johnson, stole her right out from under his buddy Brooks's nose. What a mistake. I thought Brooks would kill him with his bare hands. Brooks had a temper, and Richard deserved it."

"How did Richard wind up with Maggie?" asked Mike.

"After Nina died, he wormed his way in with Maggie. Maggie's parents were killed in a car crash. She was vulnerable. And newly rich. We all know how that turned out."

"Thanks for talking with us. Any information we gather will be useful in determining whether or not Richard gets a new trial. The overall consensus from everyone we've spoken to *except my boneheaded mother,* is that Richard was capable of murder."

Susan and Mike headed back toward their hotel.

"Are we still on for enchiladas and tacos?" said Mike.

"Si, si, Señor. *Vamos.*"

Chapter 12

Susan was happy to unzip her jeans and exchange them for pajama pants. The Mexican food was so delicious she ate until the plate was bare. Same went for Mike. *Why is it men can gorge themselves and shrug it off, while women beat themselves up the rest of the day for eating too much?* Mike had already kicked off his shoes and was relaxing on the bed, happy as a clam. A clam who'd just eaten a satisfying meal—without a bit of remorse.

"The deposition is tomorrow. That will be a big factor tipping the scales toward a new trial, don't you think?" Susan grabbed a Tums from her purse and stretched out next to Mike.

"Yeah. When do you think we'll be ready to head home?"

"The only loose end here is Jake Black. We have to find out what he's hiding," said Susan. "And I'd still like to find out Chase's last name, but at the moment I have no plan as to how to do it."

"Sleep on it. I can barely keep my eyes open."

Mike turned out the light and was soon snoring like a train. Susan crawled in beside him and fell asleep the moment her head hit the pillow. She was in the middle of a great dream involving Harrison Ford and a hammock, when she heard her name being called. She felt a hand shaking her awake.

"Susan, wake up."

"Mike? What's wrong?" She rolled over and looked at the alarm clock. "It's the middle of the night."

Mike grasped his chest. "I hurt. I can't breathe without hurting."

"Is it your heart? Are you having another heart attack?" She felt his clammy forehead and her own chest constricted.

"We have to get to the hospital. Now."

"I'll call an ambulance."

"The hospital is close. We passed it coming home. Get a taxi."

She put his jacket over his pajamas and led him into the elevator. Her mind raced. She'd almost lost him a few months ago. It was all her fault. She promised she'd watch what he ate and make him exercise. She had really dropped the ball. Badly. Her mind took her back to the ballgame... hotdogs... fries... beer. Then there was tonight. They'd gorged on fat and oil. She was sure enchiladas were made from pure lard. Or was that tamales?

A row of taxis waited outside the hotel entrance. Within minutes they were at the emergency room. She called, "Help, we need a wheelchair. He's having chest pain." Evan once told her that emergency rooms always brought patients with chest pain right to the front of the line.

Mike was immediately taken into a treatment room while Susan filled out a clipboard full of forms. *Thank God I brought the insurance card with me.* She paced in the waiting room in spite of her shaky knees. *Should I call Lynette? I should call Lynette. No, she'll just worry, and she can't do anything from New York. I'll wait and see what the doctor says first. I wish she were here. Or Evan. Evan's in medical school. He'd know what's going on.*

After what felt like an eternity, a nurse entered the waiting room. "You can come back now. The doctor is with him."

Mike looked pale and helpless lying in the treatment room. She grabbed his hand. "Mike, are you okay? Are you feeling any better?"

"Is it a heart attack? Doctor, he had a heart attack a few months ago. Did he have another one?"

"It's the first thing we checked for, and no. Fortunately his heart is just fine. It's his stomach causing him all this grief."

Mike looked at her sheepishly. "I shouldn't have eaten all those enchiladas. I just have a bad case of heartburn."

Susan felt like slapping him. "Heartburn? I…"

"Yeah, I know. I told you so. Lesson learned."

The doctor said, "We gave him antacids. He'll be fine. The nurse will be in with the discharge papers."

Susan felt her body relax for the first time since leaving the hotel room. The emergency room was hectic, but the nurse appeared promptly with the papers. Her dark hair was pulled in a bun, and flower-framed reading glasses hung from a chain around her neck. She handed Susan more forms to sign.

"The doctor left a script for more antacids in case he needs them." She handed it to Susan. As she leaned forward, Susan noticed her name tag. *No way. It's impossible. There must be dozens of people with that name. But she's a nurse. Brooks said she worked in a local hospital. I have to find out.*

"Excuse me, but I couldn't help noticing your name tag. Adair Porter; correct?" Susan's legs felt like Jell-O, waiting for an answer.

"That's me."

No way can we get this lucky. "This will seem like it's out of left field, and it is, but did you have a younger sister named Margaret?"

Adair took a step back. "Who are you? How do you know about Maggie?"

"This is going to sound completely crazy, but I'm Susan Wiles. I'm working with Brooks Churchill. You spoke with him the other day."

Adair's eyes narrowed. "Brooks who? I haven't spoken to anyone about Maggie in decades. What's this about?"

Why is she lying to us? "You know, Brooks. Curly blond hair, wire-rimmed glasses..."

"I don't know who you're talking about, and as you can see it's very busy here tonight."

"Just give me a minute. Richard Stirling may be getting a new trial. Some evidence was mishandled."

"A new trial? Over my dead body. The son of a bee killed my sister in cold blood."

A nurse from the neighboring cubicle peeked around the corner, finger to her lips, shushing her. "Adair, this is a hospital. Keep it down."

Susan lowered her volume as well. "We were under the impression you and your sister were estranged."

"We were for many years. Then I cleaned up my act, and we were on good terms. I visited her over Christmas before she was murdered."

Susan wasn't sure she heard all this correctly. Maggie and Adair were on good terms? They visited over Christmas? Was Adair lying and why? Brooks spoke to her and said she was nowhere near her sister for years before Maggie was killed.

"Adair, did you have a boyfriend named Chase? He lived across the street from your sister, right?"

"Chase's family lived down the road from Maggie and Richard. Richard's the one who hooked Chase up with the construction job down here. Had to put up with a slave driver of a boss and his sadistic, power-hungry son, but the money was good. Look, I've got to go. Patients need me."

"Mike, what's going on? That's not the story Brooks told us."

"I have no idea. Either Adair or Brooks is lying through their teeth, but why?"

Chapter 13

Susan slept in the next morning, which was a true rarity. Even after being free from the school schedule for a few years now, her internal clock had stubbornly held fast. Mike was still asleep. *He looks so peaceful. Thank God he's okay.* She jumped into the shower, planning the agenda for the day. She had to talk to Brooks about Adair, and she still hoped to find out Chase's last name. She could go back and ask Adair but sensed Adair wouldn't be open to another conversation.

Mike knocked on the bathroom door. "I ordered breakfast. Jonathan called. We're all meeting there this morning."

Susan dried off and pulled on her black yoga pants. *Even these feel tight after last night's dinner.* Room service arrived, and Susan was delighted at Mike's choice of breakfast: egg-white omelet, whole wheat toast, and half a grapefruit.

They arrived at Jonathan's office midmorning. Susan shared what she had learned from Mr. Snow about Richard.

Audrey creased her brow, displaying age lines summoned by worry. "That's not true. Richard would never have set a fire. He couldn't kill anyone. You were there, Brooks. Tell her."

Brooks said, "Richard and I left the dance early after he and Nina argued, but we went straight back to the boys' dorm. He certainly didn't set any fire."

"Mr. Snow said they found lighter fluid near the girls' dorm. The school kept it hush hush."

Brooks looked at the floor and shook his head. "No way. That's the first I've heard of lighter fluid. The fire was caused by an electrical problem. Nina's electric kettle malfunctioned. She probably went back to her room upset and tried to make herself a cup of tea. She always drank tea when she got upset."

Susan said, "So you knew Nina well? I thought Richard was seeing Maggie?"

Brooks punctuated his answer with a series of "ums" and "ughs." "It was before he and Maggie got together. Nina and I dated for a while. Then she started seeing Richard."

Susan said, "That must have upset you."

"Not really. Nina and I were already over."

Audrey added her two cents. "Brooks, it had only been a short time since you and Nina broke up. You were pretty upset."

"Maybe a little, but we were all good."

"And Richard never would have hurt Nina," said Audrey.

Susan relayed the allegations of violence Mr. Snow reported. "He said more than one student accused Richard of violence. We even talked to one, Elizabeth Wood."

Jonathan nodded. "That's right. Richard was a first-class jerk, and I'm sure he did what those girls said he did."

"Jonathan, come on. No way," said Audrey.

"Audrey, I grew up with Richard. He was a violent maniac. Even hit our mom once. Gave her a black eye. Dad beat the crap out of him for that, and he never dared touch her again."

How could two people in the same time and place view things so differently? I believe Jonathan. Audrey is blinded by her infatuation with Richard, thought Susan. She'd almost forgotten to ask Brooks about Adair in all the commotion. She relayed the conversation she'd had in the emergency room.

Brooks stared at the floor. When Susan finished, he said, "That woman is lying! How could she forget our conversation? That's crazy. Maybe she's been dipping into some of those ER drugs. She has a history, you know."

Audrey said, "Why is she lying? What is she hiding? She said she *was* at Maggie's shortly before the murder. Why would she incriminate herself?"

Jonathan said, "Yes. You'd think she'd lie about *not* being there. What Brooks said about her *not* being in New York is a perfect alibi. She said she and Maggie had made up?"

"Yes," said Susan. "She even said it was Richard who got Chase the construction job down here. Chase was practically their neighbor. He didn't live across the state."

"That woman is nuts. I don't know what her game is. I can't make any sense out of this," said Brooks.

"I wish we could get in touch with Chase," said Susan.

Jonathan flipped through the stack of papers on his desk. "Here. This is the form I got back for Chase's employment verification."

Susan read the attached note, which reiterated what Jonathan had told her on the phone. Then she noticed a paper stuck to the back. She pulled it off and held it up, then read it. "Hey, this is another verification form. The name is nice and clear."

"How does that help us?" asked Brooks.

"If someone wants verification of employment, it means he's looking for a new job, right? Adair said Chase worked for a slave-driver boss with a power-hungry son. Carl and Jake Black, no doubt."

"So?" said Brooks.

"Why does someone change jobs?"

Mike answered. "There are tons of reasons. More money, relocation, going back to school…"

"Or fighting with an employer or being unhappy in the workplace."

"What are you getting at?"

"Chances are slim, I admit," said Susan, "but if we find this person whose form we have, maybe we'll learn something. The date is recent. Maybe he can tell us something interesting about the company or about Jake Black. We could get insight into Jake Black's character and see if it convinces us he was capable of murder."

"Wow, that's a stretch even for you," said Mike.

Susan squinted at the second form. "The name is unusual. I'm sure there aren't a ton of Freedom St. Michelles in Atlanta."

Brooks said, "Go for it. We haven't got much else. Meanwhile, Audrey and I can hang out in the cafeteria over at Jake Black Construction."

Audrey jumped on the suggestion. "Brooks, that's a great idea. Maybe we'll overhear something that points us in Jake Black's direction."

Jonathan said, "At most, you'll get an idea how his employees feel about him. I'm not sure how helpful that's going to be. Anyway, I have work to do to get ready for the deposition. Axel Schumaker will be here soon."

Chapter 14

The law library was full of students. It was nearing the end of the semester, and Susan saw study groups in progress as well as individuals buried in law texts. She and Mike worked their way to the technology area. Nestled between the stacks at a chrome computer station, they found searching for Freedom St. Michelle more difficult than they'd imagined.

"Mike, when we're done, let's go back to the hospital and talk to Adair Porter. I have to know why she and Brooks tell such different stories."

"Do you really want to bother her at work? It's an emergency room. You know she'll be busy. Come to think of it, she worked the night shift. I doubt she's there this morning."

"Yeah, she wouldn't work two shifts in a row. Let's try tomorrow." Susan's eyes were drawn closer to the computer screen. She shouted, "Meanwhile, I found him!"

Two different students immersed in law tomes gave her the shush signal.

"You found Freedom?" whispered Mike.

"Yes, he volunteers for Habitat for Humanity. There's an article about a project they worked on." Her heart rate quickened.

"We still don't have an address or phone number. Wait... where is it?"

"Where's what?" asked Susan.

"Habitat for Humanity. You want to go over there, right?"

"You read my mind."

Susan and Mike hopped on MARTA and rode to the Habitat for Humanity store. Fueled by adrenaline, Susan pulled Mike into the store where several customers browsed. A middle-aged man worked behind the cashier. Behind him Susan saw a large open room full of furniture and drank in the aroma of fresh wood. An elderly gentleman worked out on the floor and approached them.

"Can I help you?"

Susan took an exaggerated breath. "Smells like someone's chopping down trees back there."

"You're close," said the worker. "We get lots of furniture donations. Couple that with a bunch of retired guys who like working with their hands and *voilà*. See that coffee table? On a slow day some of the guys build with the wood from unsalvageable pieces. Pauly over there is building a doghouse. Even brought in some of his own lumber for that."

"What a worthwhile way to spend retirement. Might do that myself in a few years. We have one of your stores in our hometown up in New York," said Mike.

"So, what can I help you with?"

"We're looking for a man named Freedom St. Michelle." Susan summoned her creative muse. "I'm on a committee to nominate community volunteers for a prestigious award. We read about Mr. St. Michelle in a recent newspaper article and feel he may be a perfect nominee." Mike rolled his eyes at her.

"Freedom works for us but not here in the store. He likes the hands-on work outdoors. We're swamped now that winter's coming. Trying to get up as many houses as possible before the cold weather sets in."

"Could I get a phone number for him?"

"Sorry, ma'am, but we can't give out that information. I'm sure you understand."

"Yes, of course. Can't be too careful these days." She exaggerated a pout while slowly turning toward the door.

"Wait. If you really want to talk to him, I know he's working on a big project over the weekend. A bunch of our guys are constructing a house behind the Walmart down the street. You might drop by there."

"Thanks," said Susan. "We'll do that." She patted herself on the back for managing to wrangle that bit of information. *I haven't lost my touch. Thank you, creative muse.*

Mike pointed out there wasn't a lot that could be done at the moment and persuaded Susan to take the afternoon off to play tourist. They ate a leisurely lunch at an Italian bistro and spent the afternoon at the Carter Center.

Chapter 15

Friday morning Susan and Mike returned to the hospital. The emergency room was calm in contrast to the beehive it had been two nights ago. The white floors glistened, and Susan detected the smell of bleach. The magazines were neatly stacked on the table in the waiting area. Susan asked the nurse at the desk if she could speak to Adair.

"I'm sorry, but Adair isn't here today."

"Can you tell me when she works next? We were here the other night—thought Mike here was having a second heart attack. He had one a few months ago. So scary. Adair Porter helped him. What an angel—sweet and reassuring. Anyhow, we wanted to drop by and thank her for what she did."

"Adair won't be back for a few weeks. She decided last minute to use her vacation time. Good for her. She never takes time off. In fact, she's always taking on extra shifts. I'll pass along that you were here. It's nice to be appreciated. We nurses don't get that a lot."

"I was a teacher my whole career. I know what you mean. Have a nice weekend."

Once outside, Susan said, "Something's fishy here. Adair decides spur of the moment to take a vacation? Two days after we talked to her? She's hiding from us."

"Don't jump to conclusions. Afraid of us? She was straightforward and sincere when we spoke to her. Wasn't at all intimidated."

"Then what? Brooks is lying? He wants nothing more than to pin Maggie's murder on someone other than Richard. It makes no sense at all. Let's catch up with Jonathan and tell him this latest development."

Outside of the hospital, Mike hailed a cab to the law school. Jonathan was working at his desk when they arrived at his office. Susan told him about Adair's disappearing act.

"Well, if we can't use her to establish reasonable doubt, all the better. Remember our goal. You and I are convinced Richard is guilty. Brooks says she was nowhere near Maggie's at the time of the murder and that they were estranged. Adair isn't here to dispute it no matter what she told you informally at the ER. If I can't find her, I can't call her as a witness for the defense. That's assuming there's a trial and that I'm the defense lawyer. It's gonna take a whole lot of convincing before I take on that role. Let's move on."

Mike said, "No one's said anything about the deposits."

"We'll delve into that further when we get to New York. We've done just about all we can here in Atlanta." Jonathan picked up a stack of papers. "We got Axel Schumaker's deposition. This is the strongest evidence we have to push for a new trial. This and the misplaced glove. I'd like to see that glove with my own eyes."

New York? I didn't realize we were all going to New York, thought Susan. *Jonathan is right. I have to remember our goal is to prevent Richard from getting a new trial while convincing Audrey and Brooks we are helping establish a defense. Jonathan reminds me of my dad. I feel a bond with him that I never felt with Audrey. Maybe I should tell him...*

The door flung open. Audrey, with Brooks trailing behind her, ran up to Jonathan and asked, "Did you get the deposition yesterday?"

"Yes, I've got it right here. Did you and Brooks get anything on Jake Black?"

"Nothing concrete. We heard some grumbling in the cafeteria—the usual stuff about too much to do, too little pay…"

Audrey asked, "Did you find Freedom St. Michelle? Or Chase?"

Susan explained Freedom's involvement with Habitat for Humanity. "Tomorrow he'll be working on a house out by Walmart. We can talk to him then."

"Don't get your hopes up, Audrey. Pinning the murder on Jake Black has a miniscule probability of working."

"Jonathan's right," said Susan. "It's all conjecture. That's what the judge will say. We have nothing to go on."

Audrey looked back and forth from Susan to Jonathan. In a tone somewhere between assertive and pleading she said, "We're not giving up."

Susan excused herself to use the restroom and was irritated when Audrey followed her down the hall. Audrey grabbed her arm. *Can't I even use the bathroom in peace?*

"Susan, you are not going to tell Jonathan you're his daughter, are you? You promised. I saw how you looked at him and how he sided with you."

"I'm going to tell him." Susan enjoyed watching the fear sweep across Audrey's face. "I'll tell him—but not in the middle of all this. You should have told him sixty-three years ago. I still can't believe you didn't." *I owe nothing to Audrey,* she thought. *If I feel the need to be honest with Jonathan sooner rather than later, so be it. Audrey and Jonathan are so different from each other. It's hard to imagine they were ever together.*

When Audrey and Susan returned, Jonathan was busily writing notes and Venn diagrams on the dry-erase board hanging behind the conference table. The left side was headed *Atlanta,* the right, *New York.* He backtracked when the women entered.

"As I was telling Brooks and Mike, here's where we stand. Here in Atlanta we found out Adair Porter went to New York around the time of Maggie's murder, but we don't know what end of the state she was at. She told Brooks she was visiting Chase's family many hours away from Maggie's house, and she hadn't talked to Maggie in years. She told Susan and Mike that she and Maggie had made up months before and she spent Christmas with her. Furthermore, she stated that Chase, her boyfriend at the time, was practically the Stirling's neighbor. She claims Richard even found Chase a job with the mall construction project here in Atlanta."

Brooks said, "I'm insulted that you think I'm lying and Adair told the truth."

"That's not what we're saying. We're just sorting out what we've gathered." Jonathan poured himself a glass of water.

Susan said, "We don't know Chase's last name, so we can't verify any of this through him. We know Adair stayed in Atlanta, went to nursing school, and got a job in a local hospital, which she's had for many years. Now she's suddenly taken off on vacation."

Brooks hit the table with his fist. "Again with verify." Jonathan ignored the comment.

"Our only other lead in Atlanta is Jake Black." Jonathan picked up the dry-erase marker and resumed writing. "Richard and his father were partners in the construction business. Richard stole from the company. The Black family went bankrupt and lost their home. Jake made a threat against Richard on TV during a news report. We are trying to gather information on Jake Black's character. Is he a person capable or likely to have committed murder? Susan and Mike will speak to his former employee, Freedom St. Michelle, to hopefully gain insight."

Brooks said, "Maggie paid back the money Richard stole. Maggie and Richard moved to New York where Richard started his own company. Maggie was into real estate. She and Richard benefitted from the housing boom in New York when two major businesses opened up."

Jonathan continued. "Jake stayed in Atlanta, and the family business rose from the ashes. He's now the head of a successful company. The question is, was he angry enough back then to follow Richard to New York? And why kill Maggie rather than Richard?"

Audrey said, "Maybe it was a mistake. He may have been waiting for Richard when Maggie surprised him by coming home first. Or he wanted to frame him."

Is she for real? thought Susan. *An intelligent woman like Audrey abandoning all reason to protect a loser like Richard Stirling. This is so sad.*

"Jake wanted to bury something. We struck a nerve asking about the incident. He doesn't want that information to surface. Why not? If he's innocent, he shouldn't feel threatened." Jonathan circled Jake Black's name on the board. "Let's dig up what more we can on Jake Black, but after the weekend let's relocate to New York. Susan and Mike, are you going to look for Freedom at the Habitat for Humanity project?"

"Mike said, "We're on it. After that, we're packing for New York."

Chapter 16

On Saturday morning Susan and Mike headed to the Habitat for Humanity site. The weather had turned colder overnight, and gray clouds threatened rain. *Mike looks hot in that Braves' sweatshirt and with that bit of stubble on his face,* Susan mused. *It's been fun working together on this case.* She kept her fingers crossed that the rain would hold off until after they met Freedom St. Michelle.

When they arrived, half a dozen men and woman were busy sawing wood, hammering, and painting. *What a worthwhile project. A family in need will have a brand new home before the holidays.* "Where do we start?" she asked.

"This way," said Mike. He led her through the grass.

"What? I can't hear you above the buzz of all those power tools."

Mike repeated himself. They approached the first volunteers they saw—a couple sanding wood.

"Excuse me," said Susan. "We're looking for Freedom St. Michelle. Can you point us in the right direction?"

"He's around the side. Tall guy wearing overalls."

They walked through wood shavings to the side of the house and spotted several men in overalls. They started with the tallest one.

"Excuse me. We're looking for Freedom St. Michelle," said Susan.

"You found him. What can I do for you?"

"We were hoping you could tell us a little about Jake Black. We understand you worked for his company."

"Jake Black? That's a strange request. Who are you anyway? Why do you want to know?"

"We want to know what kind of a boss Jake Black was. How was the atmosphere at the company? Did he treat his employees well? Any suspicious on goings?" Susan held her breath, waiting to see if Freedom would share any information.

Freedom repeated his previous question. "Why are you asking? Are you reporters?"

Susan explained the situation, being careful not to accuse Jake Black of anything. She didn't need a slander case. After a bit of convincing, Freedom responded.

"Not the best place to work. Jack Black was difficult to put it mildly. Treated his employees poorly. Piled on the work with no increase in salaries. A cheat too."

"What do you mean?"

"He was into insurance fraud. Pretended materials were stolen from sites. He asked me to drive one of his trucks into a lake so he could collect on it. That's where I drew the line. That's when I quit."

"If you had to speculate, do you think Mr. Black had it in him to murder someone?"

Freedom gave Susan a puzzled expression. "That's a strange question. I don't know. I guess you never know. Given the right circumstances, I suppose just about anyone could be pushed to the brink. Why do you ask? Does this have to do with his running for mayor?"

Susan wasn't sure she'd heard correctly. "Mayor? Jake Black is running for mayor?"

"Yeah. I'm surprised you haven't seen the signs stuck in all the yards." Raindrops began to fall, and thunder roared in the distance. "Hey, I've got to get these tools packed up before it starts pouring."

Susan and Mike thanked him and headed back to the hotel. On the way, they noticed Jake Black signs stuck in yards and even a billboard reading, "Jake Black: Take our city back."

Mike said, "It makes sense now. Jake Black is running for mayor. No wonder he doesn't want dirt from thirty years ago surfacing."

"Freedom said he was willing to dump a truck in the lake to collect the insurance. Come on. He could have killed Maggie."

"I don't think so. My take is he's a typical corporate boss. Profit's his number one priority. It doesn't make him a killer."

"Jonathan should ask him for an alibi. I want to be sure we can eliminate him from the suspect list."

"An alibi from thirty years ago? He doesn't owe us anything. We aren't the police. I think we should cross him and Adair off the list and get back to New York. If Richard gets a new trial, it's going to be because of Axel Schumaker's testimony or because of the glove."

"And if he gets a new trial, he should find another defense attorney. We all know Jonathan's heart isn't into this. I can't believe Brooks pulled the poor mother card and guilted him into investigating. I'm surprised a smart guy like Jonathan would fall for that. You didn't get your suspicious genes from him."

"Didn't get them from Audrey either. I can't believe how gullible she is. Jonathan won't agree to represent Richard."

"Then let's leave it up to Richard's possible future defense lawyer to checkout Jake Black's alibi, and call it a day."

Chapter 17

The next morning Susan and Mike ordered breakfast and began packing to leave for New York. Susan was anxious to see her daughter and granddaughter. And her cats. She missed Ludwig and Johann. She braced herself for the inevitable snubbing they'd inflict on her to show their displeasure at being left behind. Jonathan, Audrey, and Brooks would be flying back with them and staying at a nearby motel. Maggie Stirling's murder had taken place in the town of Strasburg, a little over an hour from Westbrook. This morning they would hold a planning powwow in Jonathan's office so they could hit the ground running when they got to New York.

Yesterday's storms had given way to a crisp, sunny morning. On the way to the campus, Mike and Susan passed a number of runners, bikers, and pedestrians. They were almost at their destination when Susan crinkled her nose and said, "I smell smoke."

Mike took a deep breath. "I think you're right." Two screaming fire trucks raced past them. "Looks like they're heading right to the campus."

As they got closer, gray smoke blanketed the law school. Susan coughed and pulled her sweater over her mouth and nose. A police car pulled up next to the fire trucks. A hose blasted water through a window, and firemen stormed through the front doors while a small crowd congregated in front of the building.

"Susan, Mike. Can you believe this? I got here a little while ago and found this. My office is in there!"

"Jonathan, do you know what happened?" said Susan.

"No. All we were told was to stay back. Look, there's Brooks."

Brooks ran over to them. "What's going on?" Smoke poured out of a window. Firemen were inside, and police questioned the onlookers.

When they got to Jonathan, he told them, "I was walking to my office, smelled smoke, and saw flames. The building was on fire."

"Luckily, it's a Sunday morning," said the officer. "The building was empty. This could have been much worse." The flames were dying down.

A fireman came over to them. "This fire ignited quickly. Started up there." He pointed to a window.

"That's my office!" said Jonathan. "The fire was in my office."

"Did you have a portable heater or coffeepot that may have been inadvertently left on?"

"No, neither of those."

"Anyone with reason to be in there last night or early this morning?"

"No, not that I can think of," said Jonathan.

Another fireman exited the building and came over to them. "The office is totaled. Even the filing cabinets are destroyed. Takes a lot of heat to melt through those."

Brooks asked, "Was it an electrical fire? We had those storms yesterday. Did the building get hit by lightning?"

"No, pretty sure that wasn't it. We'll be in touch after we finish our assessment. Leave us your contact information."

"All my files, my computer... all gone. Oh no! I just realized something. Axel Schumaker's deposition. It was sitting on my desk. Now it's gone."

"Is he still here?" asked Susan.

"No. He flew back to Maine last night."

Susan sympathized with Jonathan. She could only imagine how it would feel to have all your work destroyed overnight. *I'm starting to care about this man. Would I feel this bad if I didn't know he was my father?*

Audrey arrived, hair messy and lacking a jacket. "Susan? Jonathan? What's going on here? I never got a wake-up call. I got here as quick as I could."

Jonathan explained what had happened and told her to go back to her hotel. "They'll call later when they determine what caused the fire. I'll contact my insurance company."

Audrey's eyes opened wide. "You have the deposition, right? It didn't burn did it?"

"Sorry, Audrey, but it was on my desk and burned along with everything else."

"What are we going to do? Can we get him back here?"

Susan said, "Can't you see Jonathan is upset? He lost all his work in there, and all you're worried about is the deposition? All you care about is that inmate boyfriend of yours. Jonathan could have been killed. You should be thankful the fire happened when no one was in the building."

Audrey looked at the ground then up at Jonathan. "I'm sorry. Susan's right. I'm glad you're okay. New York is closer to Maine than Atlanta. We'll get Axel back for a do-over."

Susan shook her head. "Come on, Mike. Let's go back to the hotel and finish packing. Jonathan, call us when you hear from the fire department. We'll see you in New York."

Chapter 18

The flight back to New York was uneventful. Susan slept most of the way. Traffic was lighter than when they'd left for Atlanta, and soon they pulled into their driveway.

"Home, sweet home," said Mike.

Johann and Ludwig were curled up on the couch. Susan immediately meowed a hello and rubbed her face against Ludwig's soft fur. He leaped off the sofa and darted into the bedroom. The house was freezing and the refrigerator understandably bare. "Not the warm homecoming I was anticipating."

"I'll turn up the heat. Let's relax, and I'll run to the store later."

Turning on a few lights, putting on her favorite slippers, and settling down on the sofa to watch the Hallmark channel made her feel more at home. She was going to suggest ordering pizza but stopped herself, having recently renewed her vow to keep Mike's heart strong and healthy. Susan heard a key turn in the lock.

"Lynette! Annalise! I missed you both so much." She scooped Annalise into her arms. "You've grown!" Annalise kissed her with a noisy *Mmmah*.

"Mom, it's only been a few weeks."

Mike came into the living room and hugged his daughter and grandbaby.

Lynette said, "So you're ready to start investigating up here now. I sent the missing glove to the lab to check for DNA and whatever else is left after thirty years. Sounds like you eliminated the partner's son, and Maggie's sister has gone missing, right?"

"That's about where we are. We didn't explicitly eliminate Jake Black. Jonathan thinks what we overheard about 'squashing this after thirty years' has more to do with Jake's run for mayor than it does to this case. Can you use your connections to verify his alibi?"

"I'll try," said Lynette.

"We have to get Axel Schumaker here to redo the deposition. Can you believe the luck? A fire in Jonathan's office right after we have his sworn statement."

"Being in law enforcement, I've learned there are few coincidences. Like I said, I'll help however I can. I'll see if I can find anything showing Jake Black was in New York when Maggie was murdered."

"Thanks, Lynette." She was thrilled that Lynette had stopped nagging her about sleuthing, at least for the time being.

"Tell me about Jonathan. Do you like him? Does he look like you? I can't believe I'm going to meet my biological grandfather. Audrey was enough of a surprise. Is he anything like Grandpa was?"

"I have to pinch myself whenever I'm in the same room with him so I know I'm not dreaming. He's a nice man—smart, gentle. I think you'll like him, and yes, he reminds me more of Grandpa than Audrey ever reminded me of Grandma."

"Jason and I want you guys to come over for dinner tonight. I'm making zucchini lasagna."

"Sounds yummy," said Mike.

"Yummy," mimicked Annalise.

After a quick nap, Susan took a shower and got ready for dinner. Lynette knew her way around the kitchen, and both she and Mike looked forward to a home-cooked meal after all the dining out they'd been doing. Lynette and Jason lived only ten minutes away, and Susan smiled as they pulled into the driveway. She and Mike had given them the down payment for the house as a wedding gift, and she felt warm inside whenever she thought about her daughter's family enjoying the cottage-like home.

"Looks like Jason finally repaired the broken board in the fence," said Susan.

"Dollars to donuts he hired someone. Jason is one of the smartest people I know, but when it comes to tools, he has two left hands." He rang the bell. "Jason, good to see you, man. How are things over at the ivory tower?" Mike chuckled. Teasing Jason about his cushy professorship had been an ongoing joke for years.

Susan's stomach gurgled as soon as she smelled the garlic bread. She scooped up Annalise. "How's school been these days?"

Lynette said, "Much safer since you helped arrest the murderer lurking within its walls last summer. By the way, are you going back to volunteer at Westbrook High now that you're home?"

"Yes. I'll work it in around my busy schedule," said Susan. Thank God she'd fallen into solving mysteries since retirement or she'd be going crazy. "We're meeting tomorrow to plan our strategy. Can you come by? It'll give you a chance to meet Jonathan."

"I have a full load at work tomorrow, so it'll have to be another time. Are you going to check out the house where Maggie was killed? I'd start there."

"Good idea," said Susan. "We'll go there right after we meet with the others."

Susan could barely keep her eyes open during dinner. She was looking forward to sleeping in her own bed.

"Another great meal, honey. I still don't know where you learned to cook." Mike looked directly at Susan, who swatted his arm in response. "I hate to break up this party, but we should be going."

"It's good to have you back, Dad. We'll see you again soon. When are you going back to work?"

"Day after tomorrow. Looks like the clue crew will be on their own after that."

Chapter 19

The next morning Susan and Mike joined the others for a working breakfast. The hotel was across town. Susan noted that the trees had started to lose their colorful leaves, and the air was chillier than before they left for Atlanta.

"There's the Holiday Inn," said Susan. They pulled into a parking space. "This place popped up quickly. I hope it doesn't hurt the bed-and-breakfast business."

"The inn downtown is always booked. And the bed-and-breakfast near the college was full when Audrey called for reservations. We needed a new hotel."

They spotted Jonathan, Audrey, and Brooks in the lobby restaurant.

"Over here," said Brooks. "We were just starting to strategize."

Susan deliberately sat in the seat farthest from Audrey, next to Jonathan.

Brooks said, "I'm going to call Richard and get names of Maggie's friends. Then I'll see if by luck any of them are still in the area. Jonathan is going to research real estate deals that Maggie was involved in."

"Lynette suggested going by Maggie and Richard's old neighborhood. If you have an address, Mike and I will head there."

"I'll come with you," said Audrey.

That's all we need. I don't want to spend the day with her, thought Susan. "Maybe you should stay and help Jonathan."

Jonathan said, "It's okay. I've got this. Audrey can go with you."

After a quick breakfast from the buffet, the trio headed to Maggie and Richard's old place. Once in the car, Mike broke the silence. "Audrey, how has it been together with your old school friends again?"

"I don't know how you can look Jonathan in the eye," said Susan.

"Can we put this to rest, Susan? Jonathan and I were involved over sixty years ago. Do you think he wants to find out now that he had a daughter? I did him a favor. If I'd told him back then, he wouldn't have gone on to law school. I don't think he wants to know. If he thought it through, he could put the pieces together."

"You're saying Jonathan is denying he could have had a child? He told me he desperately wanted children and it's one of his biggest regrets that he didn't have any."

"Susan, you can't turn back time. You had loving parents. You found your birth mother. Just let sleeping dogs lie."

Susan felt the heat rise in her chest. "When we're done with this Richard Stirling thing, I'm going to tell him that I'm his daughter." Mike gave her a sideways glance.

"When we're done, do whatever you want," said Audrey. "I thought you'd handle this with more maturity. Instead, you sound like a spoiled child."

"Here we are," said Mike. He parked the car and jumped out to open Audrey's door. They stood at the curb, staring at the house.

"Now what?" said Mike. "What exactly are we looking for?"

Audrey said, "Let's knock on the door."

"That's a stupid idea," said Susan. "Whoever lives there now wouldn't have known Maggie and Richard.

Maggie would have been dead and Richard in jail when the house was sold."

"Do you have a better idea?" Audrey asked.

Mike said, "Let's knock on the neighbor's door. There's a car in the driveway. Let's start there."

Mike led the way to the brick house next door. An elderly woman answered, and Mike explained what they were after.

"No, I never knew them. We moved here twenty years ago, and they were long gone."

"Do you know which neighbors might have been here back then?"

"The couple on the other side. They were here when we moved in. They might remember them."

They thanked her and walked to the other side of the Stirlings' house where they found a woman in a Yale sweatshirt raking leaves in the backyard.

"Excuse me," said Susan. "We're looking for someone who may have known Maggie and Richard Stirling."

"Oh, my! Maggie and Richard Stirling. Haven't heard those names in years." The woman put down the rake and sighed. "What a tragedy. Maggie and I were friends. I was heartbroken when she was murdered. That son-of-a-bee husband of hers killed her, you know."

Audrey, arms tightly crossed over her chest, said, "As a matter of fact, he didn't kill her. Evidence was mishandled, and he's going to get a new trial."

Susan rolled her eyes at Audrey. Mike grabbed her hand and squeezed.

"Really? That's news to me after all these years."

"They're looking at other suspects. Can you tell me if you think anyone else had it in for Maggie?" asked Audrey.

Susan said, "She means, do you remember anyone suspicious around the neighborhood, or did Maggie mention having problems with anyone? At work maybe."

"As a matter of fact, Maggie got some flower deliveries. Once she was at work and I was home sick, so the FTD man left a bouquet for me to give her. When I gave them to her later, she threw them in the trash. I asked her what was wrong, and she said she didn't want to talk about it."

"Could they have been from her husband?"

"No, I doubt it. Maggie and Richard weren't getting along. Maggie was talking divorce. Anyhow, Richard wasn't the flower-giving type."

Audrey said, "I know Richard. I'd disagree with that."

"He was a charmer," said the neighbor. "but Maggie saw his true colors."

Mike stepped between Audrey and the neighbor. "Anything else unusual?"

"Well, there was that incident."

"What incident?" Three pairs of eyes stared at her.

"The spray-painting incident. A few weeks before she died, someone spray-painted all over their front door."

"Did it say anything?" said Susan.

"It said 'you'll pay.' It was written in red paint. Big letters. The police came and took pictures. The next day my husband helped Richard repaint the door."

"Did Maggie say who she thought did it?"

"No, but she was very upset. If you'll excuse me, I need to get ready for a doctor's appointment. You can talk to the people across the street. They've lived here even longer than me."

On their way across the street, they passed a woman walking a dog. Susan stopped her to ask about the Stirlings.

"The Stirlings. The haunted house? The place was for sale when we moved in. Can you believe the realtor neglected to tell us a murder had taken place in there? Good thing we found out when we did. Fired him right away and bought our place down the street."

"Haunted?" said Susan.

"Yeah. After the murder, people saw lights turning on and off at odd hours. There were rumors of a dark-haired woman lurking around outside. Gives me the shivers just thinking about it."

When they were out of the neighbor's earshot, Susan said, "Haunted? What do you make of that?"

"I think she's looney," said Mike. "Someone lives there now, right? We already heard about the dark-haired woman, and during the investigation and resale of the house, lights would have been going on and off. I'd ignore her."

They continued to the house across the street, which sported yellow aluminum siding, white shutters, and black numbers alongside the storm door. Mike rang the doorbell, which was answered by an older couple. Again they explained what information they were seeking. The gray-haired woman in the wool sweater and the bald gentleman wearing a Jets sweatshirt invited them inside to sit down.

"I saw a delivery van there a few times," said the gentleman. "Flowers delivered. You don't see that much on our street. We all grow our own flowers. Don't need to go buying those fancy, expensive *arrangements*."

"Speaking of flowers, one day Maggie's mums in front of her front door were all dug up. She was pretty upset. No way that happened naturally," said the woman.

Susan said, "Did you see any strangers hanging around the house ever?"

"Yes, a dark-haired woman. Stylish clothes, short, expensive haircut. Saw her a few times going into the place when Maggie was there and a few times looked like she was sneaking around when no one was home. Oh, and after the murder, I saw her looking in the windows one night."

Audrey said, "Did she drive a green van?"

"Oh, no. She had a sporty little green thing. Not a van."

On the way back to the hotel, Susan considered what they'd learned. Maggie got flower deliveries, which she wasn't happy about. Someone sprayed graffiti all over her front door and dug up her mums. A stylish, dark-haired woman visited several times and was also seen sneaking around the house both before and after the murder. A lot to think about. Was there actually another suspect? Or two? Could Richard be innocent after all?

Chapter 20

Susan and Mike pulled into the Holiday Inn. Jonathan had reserved a conference room behind the lobby, and once settled, Brooks and Jonathan reported what they'd found.

"I talked to Richard and got the names of three of Maggie's friends," said Brooks. "One is dead. Cancer. Another lives about an hour from here. I called, and she said she'd meet with us this evening. The third was a coworker. I haven't been able to locate her."

Jonathan said, "I looked into the real estate records. Maggie sold a ton of houses in what was then a brand new development near the Ford plant. I tracked down the name of the builder. Maggie and he had a contract. He built the houses; she had exclusive selling rights."

"Did you talk to him?" said Susan.

"Here's the weird part," replied Jonathan. "The man had a booming business. Couldn't build houses fast enough to keep up with the demand. A few months after the trial, the guy goes and jumps off a bridge. Doesn't make any sense."

"Very strange," said Mike. "Do you think he's the one who was sending flowers?"

"I don't know. Maybe when we talk to Maggie's friend tonight she can answer that," said Susan.

After making plans to meet later on, Susan and Mike headed home. Susan changed into her favorite yoga pants and a velour sweatshirt. She noticed two new messages on her phone. The first was from Westbrook High. The media specialist wanted to find out if she was still returning to volunteer the next day. Susan missed her friends at the school. Volunteering was way more fun than teaching had been. She had the time to gossip and order out for lunch—things she could never do as a teacher. Next she called Lynette.

"Mom, I wanted to let you know I checked into Maggie's financial records. There were a series of large deposits made into her savings account at regular intervals. I couldn't trace where they were from."

"Were they commission checks? We found out she sold a lot of houses back then."

"If that were the case," replied Lynette, "the amounts would have varied. Commissions are based on a percentage of the sale price. Also the deposits wouldn't have been made at regular intervals. If she was able to sell houses on schedule like that, she would have written a best-selling book, or at least she would have won a realtor-of-the-year trophy."

"What then? Bribes? Was she skimming money?"

"Skimming money off her own business? I don't think so. If she was taking bribes, for what? Who was paying her and for what?"

"We're meeting one of her friends tonight. I'll ask if she has any ideas."

Susan cooked stir-fried chicken and vegetables for dinner. Since the heart attack scare back in Atlanta, Mike hadn't been objecting at all to eating a healthier diet. She slipped a bit of her chicken to Ludwig and Johann, hoping to make up for the time away. After dinner, she packed the leftovers for Mike's lunch, then retrieved his clean clothes from the dryer and brought the basket upstairs.

"Susan, are you ready? We're supposed to pick up the rest of the crew at the hotel in a little while."

"I'm coming."

Mike picked up Jonathan and Audrey outside the hotel entrance.

"Where's Brooks? Isn't he coming?" asked Susan.

"Brooks is staying behind to search for Maggie's other friend," said Jonathan.

The mountain roads were dark and deserted, but Mike knew them like the back of his hand, and they arrived safely at their destination.

Virginia Small, a robust blonde with wrinkled hands and a warm smile, lived in a farm house complete with a barn and silo. Susan guessed she was in her seventies. *I hope I look as young as she does ten years from now.* Susan introduced the group, and they followed Virginia into the living room. A fire crackled in the fireplace, and the sofa was draped in a colorful crocheted afghan.

"Thanks for seeing us, Virginia," said Susan.

"Please, call me Ginny. When Mr. Churchill told me you were looking into Maggie's murder, I told him I'd do anything I could to help. I miss Maggie to this day. She was a one-of-a-kind friend."

"Ginny, is there anyone besides Richard who may have wanted Maggie dead? Did she tell you anything about receiving flowers or having her property vandalized?"

"Yes, Susan. Maggie didn't want to talk about it, but she told me someone had been stalking her. She didn't know for sure, but she suspected the guy who delivered supplies to her real estate office. She said he gave her the creeps."

"Do you know his name?" asked Audrey.

"Dear me, no. I have trouble remembering what I ate for breakfast these days. I'm sure it's in with her office records."

"Surely the office isn't still in existence," said Jonathan.

"I can't say for sure. She had taken on a partner, a young guy fresh out of school. Maybe you can track him down. Richard would know his name. He's the one who introduced them."

"Anything else you can tell us?" asked Susan.

"There were those cryptic phone calls. Twice when I was over at her house, she went into the bedroom to talk. Asked me to hang up the phone when she got to the extension. I wasn't eavesdropping, mind you, but it was a woman's voice. I asked Maggie about it, but she said I was better off not knowing."

"Did she seem scared or upset afterward?"

"No, not at all."

"Thank you for your time," said Susan. "I'll jot down my number. Call if you think of anything else."

A light rain fell as they got back into the car. Susan yawned and rested her head against the car door.

Mike said, "For a woman who can't remember what she ate for breakfast, I'd say she gave us a lot of information."

"Are you going to find out if the real estate office still exists?" asked Audrey. "I'm going to call Richard myself and find out what he knows."

"Good luck getting through to him at the prison," said Susan. She closed her eyes.

"Calm down, Audrey. The whole partner thing has a lot of contingencies," said Jonathan. "It's probably another dead end just like Chase and Freedom St. Michelle."

Audrey huffed and crossed her arms tightly.

Mike said, "It'd be more efficient to ask Lynette to look into stalking incidents from around that time."

From out of nowhere a car whizzed by on the two-lane mountain road, nearly clipping the door of Susan's Prius. "What was that?" Susan, who'd been on the verge of falling asleep, was suddenly wide-awake.

The car made a U-turn and came back at them head on, bright headlights glaring, blinding Mike.

"What the heck?" Mike swerved into the other lane, narrowly avoiding the other car. The drizzle had made the road slippery, and Susan held her breath as Mike straightened out the Prius.

"He must be drunk," said Audrey. "Call the police."

"He's gone now. Drunk drivers aren't so proficient at making U-turns on slippery mountain roads. He was targeting us," said Mike. "The question is *why.*"

Chapter 21

Susan tossed and turned all night. *Who would want to harm us?* She would call Lynette in the morning. Before she knew it, sunlight streamed through the window. *It's already time to get ready for school. I'm going to need a nap later.* Mike had already showered and was eating an egg-white omelet when she came downstairs.

"Close call last night," she said.

"We must have hit on something that someone doesn't want us to find out. Richard may be innocent after all. Be careful. Don't go off snooping on your own."

"The only place I'm going today is Westbrook High. The kids *have* gotten tougher these days, but I can hold my own. Don't forget your lunch."

Mike kissed her good-bye. She cleaned up the breakfast dishes and headed to the school.

Westbrook High was a clean, two-story building where most of the students had been together since kindergarten, and the majority of the faculty had taught the parents of the current student body. Janet, the media specialist, gave her a standing ovation when she walked into the library. Students filled the computer desks, and a few teachers were browsing the stacks and DVDs.

"I really missed you. Look at that stack of books to be shelved. And we just got in a new order of Biology textbooks to check in." Janet smiled. "More importantly, I'm craving some good gossip!"

"Never fear, help is here!" *It's nice to be needed.* "I'll get right to work."

"Tell me about Atlanta first. Did you meet your birth father? What's he like?"

"He's very nice."

"Nice? That's the most descriptive adjective you could come up with? What did he say when he found out you were his daughter?"

"I didn't tell him. Not yet anyway. We have to focus on Richard's case, and it's complicated with Audrey around. I'm so mad at her for keeping him from me."

"It has to be hard. I'd tell him if I were you. Has Lynette met him?"

"Not yet. She's dying to, but she's been busy with work."

"Are you still investigating? Your parents came back here with you, right?"

My parents. Still doesn't feel natural to hear or say those words.

"Yes. Jonathan and Audrey are both here. Me and my birth parents. One happy little family."

Susan grabbed a cart and began rounding up the random books left on the tables after the morning bell rang. She did her best thinking while cleaning. *If Lynette finds the stalker, that could be the answer. But who is the dark-haired woman with the sports car? And where did Maggie get the deposits from?* She took a break and sat at one of the computers. *Maybe I can find out about the builder Maggie worked with. The one who mysteriously killed himself after the trial.* She calculated the approximate date but realized she'd be better off with microfiche considering the event took place so long ago.

"Hi, Susan. Glad you're back."

Susan turned around. "Julie, it's nice to see you too."

"You look frustrated. What information are you looking for? Janet told me you were out of town investigating the Stirling case. Do you really think he's innocent?"

"No, but he deserves a fair shot being the evidence was mishandled. Did you ever hear about a builder who killed himself shortly after Richard's trial? I don't know his name, but I know Maggie worked with him, selling the houses he built. Never mind. It was way before your time."

"I do remember hearing about it. I wonder if he's the one who was blamed for the contaminated water. It was a huge scandal. I know because the teacher next door to me, Debbie Carlise, bought a house in a brand new development across the river when she moved here. Must be around thirty years ago. She came here as a new teacher and will be retiring at the end of the year. That's around thirty years I'd guess."

"Tell me what you know."

"Debbie moved here when her husband got a job with IBM. They had a son who developed cancer."

"Is he still alive?"

"Yes. He beat the cancer, but several kids in the neighborhood also became ill, and not all of them were so lucky. Hey, there's Debbie now. Might as well go to the primary source. Debbie, come over here." She waved to a woman who smiled and joined them.

"Susan, right?" said Debbie. "I've seen you in here before."

Julie said, "Susan is a super sleuth. She helped clear my fiancé, Tank, of some serious charges not long ago. Now she's working on the Richard Stirling case. Tell her about the cancer thing that happened in your neighborhood."

"It feels like it was yesterday. My little boy got very sick. There was an unusually high incidence of children diagnosed with cancer in our development. I talked to those mothers, and we came to the conclusion it wasn't a coincidence. First thing we did was get the water tested. Bingo. High levels of toxic chemicals were being dumped into the water supply by the new factory down the road."

"What happened then?"

"A group of us got together. My neighbor, Frank Paglieri, organized us. His son had leukemia and later died. We tried to sue the builder, but we lost in court. The company dumping the chemicals got heavily fined. They had to pay to clean up the water supply, but the families going through this got nothing in the way of compensation for medical bills or pain and suffering."

"I'm sorry you had to go through that," said Susan. "Companies think they're above the law sometimes."

"Yes, but we blamed the builder. We're sure he *knew* he was building on top of a sewer pool."

The bell rang, and both teachers hustled back to their classrooms. Susan was left alone with her thoughts. *The builder kills himself even though the court found him innocent. Suddenly his conscious bothers him? Maggie sold those houses. Did she know about the polluted water supply? If so, she made herself a target.*

Deciding this required more research, Susan located the articles she needed and sat down in the back of the library with the antiquated microfiche reader. *Eight children developed cancer during that time period. Four of them died. This other article says a group of parents led by Frank Paglieri sued the builder and lost the case.* She scrolled through pages of articles, finding no mention of Maggie. She found an article about the builder's death. *The builder, Thomas Crow, died under mysterious circumstances. They called it a suicide but mentioned the objections raised by his family.*

According to his wife, he never would have jumped off the Hudson Bridge. He was afraid of heights.

Janet leaned over her shoulder. "All done shelving?"

Susan looked around at the half-full cart. "No, I'm sorry. I got distracted. Do you remember this case where the builder of Debbie's development killed himself?"

"Yes, Thomas Crow. It was big news since suicides and murders rarely happen near Westbrook. At least they didn't before you moved here." She smiled at Susan. "The builder's daughter works here you know."

Not believing the coincidences she'd lately encountered, Susan said, "Are you kidding? What does she teach?"

"She's not a teacher. She's one of the secretaries in the guidance department. Anna. Anna Cabrini. She was just a baby when it happened."

"Do you mind if I take a stroll down to guidance?"

"Go for it, Sherlock."

Susan checked the guidance department and found that Anna Cabrini had called in sick. She resigned herself to waiting until Thursday to talk to her when she'd next be volunteering. Susan returned to the media center for a few hours. By the time she left, every stray book was back on its shelf.

Chapter 22

"Lynette, I'm on my way home. Guess what I found out at school today? Maggie worked with a Thomas Crow who built the development near the Ford plant. Toxic waste was being dumped into the water supply, and Crow knew about it. Cases of childhood cancer popped up in unusually large numbers. Residents led by a father named Frank Paglieri got together and tried to sue Tom Crow and Maggie, but lost the case. Frank's son died from leukemia."

"Slow down. Are you saying this Frank Paglieri was so angry about losing the case that he murdered Maggie Stirling?"

"Maggie sold him the house. Thomas Crow swore he wasn't aware he was building homes over toxic waste. The court agreed with him."

"And?"

"Thomas Crow jumped off the Hudson Bridge. Committed suicide even though he was exonerated."

"Guilt can be a powerful force."

"Thomas Crow was deathly afraid of heights. I read that in a newspaper article. They quoted his wife. She said a) he was not depressed and felt he'd done nothing wrong, b) he owned a gun, and if he were to kill himself, he'd have used it rather than climbing up a bridge, and c) he didn't leave a suicide note."

Susan pulled her car into a McDonald's drive-through. She'd been craving a Big Mac, and as she wasn't with Mike, here was her opportunity.

"Mom, what's that sound?"

"Just the radio."

"Since when does the radio ask if it can help you? You're ordering junk food, right? Let me guess. McDonald's."

"Boy, I'm continually impressed with your detective skills. Everything in moderation. Besides, I'm not the one who had a heart attack. It's not like I'm doing this in front of Dad."

Susan arranged the bag of food on the passenger seat and grabbed a handful of fries before she pulled out to the main road.

"Those deposits into Maggie's account may have been bribes to keep quiet. That means she knew what was going on. I'll track down Frank Paglieri."

After thinking it through, Susan neglected to tell Lynette about being chased off the road the previous night. Lynette only accepted her sleuthing because Susan had assured her she wouldn't put herself in danger. If she put herself in danger unintentionally, did that count? She figured Lynette would think so. When she pulled into her neighborhood, she saw Mike's car in the driveway.

"Mike, how was your first day back?" She gave him a hug.

"Good. They managed fine without me. What about yours?"

Susan shared the new information she'd learned. After dinner, they sat down at the computer and researched cases of companies that had been sued for illegally dumping toxic waste.

"Costs them a pretty penny to properly dispose of the stuff," said Mike. "Even more when the company is sued and then has to pay to clean up their mess. Here's a similar case. Fairly recent. Both the builder and the real estate agency were sued because residents found lead in their water."

Susan's phone vibrated on the table. "It's Jonathan."

"Yes, that's what I suspected. Both the builder and Maggie were sued, and neither was found guilty. I know. Nowadays they wouldn't have gotten away with it. I talked to a teacher at school who lived there. Her son and several other neighborhood kids got cancer."

Mike brewed a cup of coffee while waiting for Susan to finish her phone call. Then he sat down and turned on *Jeopardy*. By the time Susan finished the call, Alex was announcing the final *Jeopardy* category.

"Well? What did Jonathan have to say?"

"He agrees that Frank Paglieri, the one who lost his son to cancer and organized the parents to sue, had motive for killing both Maggie and the builder, Tom Crow. The circumstances of Crow's suicide were suspicious, even though the coroner found no evidence of foul play. He thinks we should talk to Paglieri."

"We? He thinks you should go talk to a suspected murderer?"

"Not exactly. He thinks Lynette should talk to him. But I'm the one who found out about the cancer cases. I should go along."

"See what Lynette has to say about that."

"And by the way, Axel Schumaker will be here tomorrow. I know you're working, but the rest of us are going to meet after breakfast." She turned to the TV.

"Hah, I was right," announced Mike. "Who is Erin Brokovich? I just won us 40,000 dollars."

Chapter 23

Susan fed Johann and Ludwig, then grabbed her jacket and made her way to the hotel. She was glad Axel Schumaker had agreed to redo the deposition after the last one had been burned in the fire back in Atlanta. Today they would talk with him before the official deposition and see if his memory could be further jogged. Would he remember more details this time? Did he see a dark-haired lady in a sports car lurking around the neighborhood? Or a stalker bearing flowers?

The clue crew met in the hotel conference room. Susan couldn't imagine Jonathan taking a deposition here. *Maybe Lynette can get a room at the station*, she thought. *Then she can lock the tape away in a police vault. A fireproof vault so it stays safe.* Susan sat down next to Jonathan.

"Susan, we were just getting started," said Jonathan. "I was asking Mr. Schumaker if he remembered seeing flower deliveries or anyone suspicious in the neighborhood. Mr. Schumaker, would you hand me the green folder."

"Sure. Here you go."

"No, not the red one, the green one."

Axel said, "Oops. I do that all the time. Here's the green folder."

Doesn't know his colors? Susan thought. *Boy he's going to make a great witness. I hope he at least cleans up well. Wait, no I don't. I have to remember I don't want Richard to get a new trial.*

Axel gulped his coffee. "I saw the FTD van next door a couple of times. Don't remember seeing anyone suspicious. The house next door got sprayed up pretty bad with graffiti one time. My parents were upset. Thought it was one of the neighborhood kids. Told me if I ever did something like that I wouldn't be able to sit down for a week."

Susan's mind wandered again. *Tell us something we don't already know. He was just a kid. I don't know what we expected to hear beyond the green van and the partial description of the driver the night of Maggie's murder.*

Jonathan said, "Were there other cars that came into the neighborhood regularly that didn't belong to the people in your development?"

Axel scratched his beard. "Don't think so." He took another swig of coffee. "Wait, maybe. There was this little green car sometimes parked in the Stirling's driveway. Once I saw it pull in late at night after I came back from the Pinewood Derby contest down at the school. I won, you know. Parents took me and some of my scout friends out to Friendly's for ice cream. When we got back I remember my parents saying something about who was over there late at night while Mr. Stirling was out of town. Mama said maybe there was some hanky-panky going on."

"Did you ever see the driver?"

"No. Not that night. But once before, I did see a lady get out of that car and knock on the side door. Mrs. Stirling opened it for her. I was raking leaves outside."

Jonathan said, "Do you remember what she looked like?"

Brooks leaned forward. "You wouldn't remember after all these years, right?"

"I remember she had one of those cute short haircuts. Looked like that Olympic skater. She was thin, short, tight jeans."

"Thanks, Mr. Schumaker. We'll get together tomorrow for the deposition. I'll call you with the time and place." Jonathan shook his hand.

Audrey jumped up. "See. There's another suspect. A dark-haired lady in a green car. We have to ask Richard about it."

"The neighbor already mentioned the dark-haired lady. That information isn't new," said Susan.

"Can't ask Richard," said Brooks. "Prison is on lockdown. No visitors. No calls either."

Jonathan said, "Is this about those cons who escaped weeks ago? Haven't they caught them yet?"

"Nope. And they think one of the workers at the prison may have been involved. We won't be able to talk to Richard yet."

Susan volunteered to go by the station and arrange a place for the deposition. She was also hoping to set up a time for Lynette to meet Jonathan. *I know Lynette is going to like him. Maybe if things work out, Evan will be able to meet him too.*

After leaving the deposition, she went straight to the police station. As soon as she walked in, she saw her old buddy, Lynette's partner, Jackson Simpson.

"Hey there, Miss Marple. Long time no see. How was Atlanta?"

"Not bad, but it's always good to be home. How's Theresa? She feeling okay?"

"The usual pregnancy complaints. She's tired, her back hurts, but yeah, she's great. Just a few more months, and we'll be parents."

"Did you find out the sex? Last time I asked Lynette she said you didn't know."

"We're having a little boy." His smile lit up the room.

Susan pictured a little dark-haired, beer-bellied son. She squeezed the image from her mind. "Hope he looks like Theresa."

"Very funny. Theresa's looks and my smarts. What a combination that would be. Gonna be one heck of a kid."

Lynette opened her office door. "Hey, Mom. Come on in." Lynette checked the schedule. "We can do the deposition at ten tomorrow morning."

"Great. Do you want to go to lunch?"

"Sure. I've got a light schedule this afternoon."

"Lynette, I had an idea. Let me call Jonathan and see if he can eat with us. I really want you to meet him."

"That would be great."

Susan called Jonathan, and they swung by the hotel to pick him up on the way to lunch.

"Jonathan, this is my daughter, Lynette."

Jonathan shook her hand, and Susan got goose bumps watching him meet his granddaughter for the first time. She sensed an immediate connection between the two as they chatted in the car.

According to Lynette, The Downtown Deli served the best bagel sandwiches around. It was bustling with the lunch crowd, but they didn't have to wait long before being seated at a diner-style booth. Lynette got the bagel burger with a half sour pickle.

"I'll have what she's having," said Jonathan.

Susan ordered pastrami on an onion bagel.

"Mom, I have some news about Jake Black. We verified his alibi for the night Maggie was murdered. He was in Atlanta. We can cross him off the list."

"I guess Mike was right. He was protecting his run for mayor. I have a new clue. Frank Paglieri. He led the losing lawsuit against Maggie and the builder, Tom

Crow. I was thinking of paying him a visit. According to my source at Westbrook High, he still lives in the same place as he did back then. He couldn't afford to leave the neighborhood. After the contaminated water became headline news, the housing values plummeted."

"Are you nuts? He could be a raving, shotgun-toting lunatic for all you know. You're not going out there."

"She's right," said Jonathan.

"Maybe I shouldn't go… alone. Didn't you say your schedule today was light, Lynette?"

Lynette rolled her eyes at her mom. Then she turned to Jonathan. "She does this to me all the time. I either agree to go with her, or she'll go alone in spite of my misgivings." She looked at Susan. "Sure. Let's go."

They dropped Jonathan off at the hotel. Susan was eager to hear Lynette's opinion of her grandfather.

"He seems very nice. Smart, caring. I'm looking forward to getting to know him better. You are going to tell him you're his daughter, right?"

"Yes, very soon."

Orchard Drive was less than an hour away. They crossed the river, passed the Ford plant, and came to a residential area. Most of the houses were two story, some covered with weathered aluminum siding, others brick. They pulled into a driveway with a hand-painted sign reading "The Paglieris" hanging from the mailbox.

"Can I help you?" A plump woman wearing an apron opened the door. Susan smelled the delightful aroma of simmering tomato sauce.

Lynette showed her badge. "We have a few questions. A case from thirty years ago may be reopening. We're gathering information. Is your husband home?"

"Frank!" The woman yelled up the stairs, and Frank Paglieri shuffled down them and into the living room.

His stature was slight. His gray hair and slouching posture made him appear to be much older than his wife. Lynette asked him about the night Maggie was killed.

"Again they're asking me this? Yeah, I was mad. Yeah, I wanted to kill the people responsible for our son's death. But I didn't. I'm a church-going man, always have been. I figured that builder and the woman who sold us the house would rot in hell. I'm sure that's where they are."

"Did you give the police an alibi?" asked Lynette.

The wife spoke up. "The night that realtor was killed, my husband and I had driven down to New Jersey to visit friends. They're no longer alive, God rest their souls. We told all this to the police. Don't they keep records?"

"I have it in the police report, but it says they never tracked down those friends."

"That's because they left for an extended trip to Europe the very next day. That's why we went to visit—to send them off." The woman wrung her hands as she spoke.

Lynette continued. "What about the night Tom Crow jumped off the bridge? Do you remember that night, Mr. Paglieri?"

"I told the police I was home with my wife."

"That's right. He was here all evening." Her eyes darted back and forth between Lynette and Susan.

Lynette thanked them, and she and Susan got back into the car.

Once they were on the road, Susan said, "That woman was lying. Did you notice how uncomfortable she looked?"

"I sure did. If we find out what it is she's hiding, we may be closer to having an alternate suspect."

Chapter 24

Susan got ready to go into Westbrook High. Number one on her agenda was stopping at the guidance office to speak with Anna Cabrini. *Paglieri was home with his wife the night Tom Crow died. That was his alibi anyway. His wife acted nervous when she vouched for his whereabouts. Did Anna Cabrini think Paglieri murdered her father or that Tom Crow actually committed suicide?*

Susan opened the glass door to the guidance department. She saw a few parents waiting for conferences and a few students lined up at the front counter, presumably asking questions or scheduling appointments. The two desks behind the counter were occupied. On the right, a young woman who could pass for a student held a phone to her ear. At the desk on the left, a pretty blonde typed at her computer. She looked up at Susan.

"May I help you?"

"Yes, I'm Susan Wiles. I volunteer upstairs in the media center. Do you have a few minutes?"

"Sure. Come have a seat." Susan entered through the gate in the front counter.

"I'm looking for information about the death of Maggie Stirling. She was the realtor who worked with your father thirty years ago. She and your father died the same year under questionable circumstances. Maggie was murdered by her husband... that's what the jury determined. I hear there was controversy over how your father died."

Anna looked at the floor. "My mom said it was murder. My father was afraid of heights. He never would have climbed up the bridge and jumped off."

"What does *she* think happened?"

"You mean what *did* she think? My mom died last year."

"I'm so sorry. I lost my mom not too long ago. I miss her every day."

"Why are you asking about this now?"

"Richard Stirling, Maggie's husband, may be granted a new trial. We're trying to come up with alternate suspects. I'm exploring a connection between your father's death and Maggie Stirling's. They were both unsuccessfully sued by a resident of your father's housing development over the contaminated water."

"I was just a kid when all that happened, but my father was a strong man. He wouldn't have taken his own life, leaving me, my mom, and my sister alone."

The phone on her desk rang. While she answered it, Susan noticed the office had cleared out now that the school day was in session. Anna reminded her of Lynette.

"Can I help you with anything else, Mrs. Wiles?"

"No. Thank you for talking to me. If you remember anything relevant, I volunteer in the media center every Tuesday and Thursday."

Susan spent a few hours in the media center then went to pick up Axel Schumaker, who she'd volunteered to bring to the police station for the deposition. She pulled in front of his hotel, where they'd agreed to meet. *I'm ten minutes late. He should be out here already.* She tried calling his room. When he didn't answer, she parked and went into the lobby. *We're going to be late. I told Lynette we'd be there at ten. Where is he?* She fidgeted with her keys as she walked up to the front desk.

"Excuse me, I'm supposed to be meeting someone, and he hasn't come down. Would you mind trying his room?"

The front desk worker tried the room. "He's not answering."

"Can you send someone in to see if he's there?"

"No, ma'am. We aren't permitted to do that."

Susan paced, looking at her watch every few minutes. *I'll call Lynette. I hope we don't lose the conference room.* Lynette reassured her that the room would still be available. Then she put Jonathan on the phone.

"Susan, where could he have gone? We're all set up here. Try him again."

Susan tried again, but Axel still didn't answer. She went up to his room and knocked on the door. "Axel, are you there? It's Susan. I'm going to take you to give the deposition." She knocked more aggressively. "Axel, open up." Her knuckles hurt from knocking. *What now? Think, Susan.* She spotted the cleaning cart coming toward her and got an idea. She put her hand on the doorknob, pretending it was her room.

When the cleaning woman passed, she said, "Oh, dear me. I just closed the door and I left my key inside. Would you open it for me so I don't have to go all the way back down to the front desk." She rubbed her hip. "I'm still recovering from my surgery. It hurts like the dickens when I walk too much."

Her performance convinced the cleaning lady to open the door.

"Thank you so much. I'll be sure to tell the management how kind you were to this old lady."

When the cleaning woman went on with her work and entered the next room, Susan walked into Axel's room, calling his name. Then she saw him. On the floor. Next to the bed. A bullet hole in his back. She screamed.

Oh, my God. There's blood all over! He has to be dead. Oh dear Lord! She screamed, "Help, help! Come quick. There's a body on the floor, help!"

The cleaning woman came running back and entered the room. "Oh my God, is he dead?"

Susan screamed, "Get the manager! Call the police! Call 911."

The cleaning woman ran to the elevator and pounded the button. After what seemed like an eternity, she returned with the manager, who looked at the body, gasped, and took a step backward.

"Call the police," said Susan." Don't touch anything." Her hands trembled.

"Already done. Do you know this man?"

"I-I do. His name is Axel Schumaker. He's from Maine."

Her legs shook while she and the hotel manager stood over the body, waiting for help to arrive. She thought, *No one heard a gunshot? The room looks undisturbed. His wallet is still there on the nightstand. There's no sign of forced entry as far as I can see. Someone wanted to make sure Axel Schumaker never got the chance to give his deposition. Was the same person responsible for the fire in Jonathan's Atlanta office?*

When the police arrived, they secured the scene and escorted Susan and the manager out of the room. Lynette ran out of the elevator.

"Mom, what happened?"

"It's Axel. He's dead. I was supposed to pick him up…"

"I know. I was waiting for you at the station when we got the call. Did you see anyone leaving the room?"

"No. I kept calling the room. Then I came up here and knocked on the door. No one answered, so I went in."

"Mom, the door was unlocked?"

"Not exactly. The cleaning lady let me in. Who would have wanted Axel dead? Who even knew he was in town?"

Susan watched the paramedics and coroner enter Axel's room. Her heart was pounding.

"Come on, Mom. Let me bring you to the station if you're up to it so you can give an official statement. Are you okay?"

"A little shaken up, for sure."

Lynette put her arm around her and led her downstairs.

Chapter 25

I'm feeling too old for all this excitement, Susan thought. *Most people go through their entire lives never seeing a dead body. Why is it I've been so unlucky? I hope Mike gets here soon.*

"Mom, they're processing the crime scene. Did you tell anyone outside of the clue crew about the deposition?"

"No. I did mention to the Paglieris that the case may be reopened."

"We'll talk to them. Anyone else?"

"No. I may have told Anna Cabrini, the builder's daughter we were investigating, but she'd have no reason to go after Axel. What about the stalker? Or the dark-haired woman with the Dorothy Hamill haircut? Or Adair?"

"We tracked down Adair. She's on a cruise in the Bahamas. Won't be back for weeks."

Mike, out of breath, burst into Lynette's office and hugged Susan. "Are you okay? I can't believe Axel was murdered."

Lynette took a phone call while Mike comforted his wife. "That was the lab," she reported. "They found traces of accelerant on the glove found at the crime scene where Maggie was murdered."

"But there was no fire when Maggie was murdered. What does it mean?" asked Susan.

"I don't know yet. It's another piece of the puzzle. Go home. Relax, it's been a stressful day."

Mike put his arm around Susan and took her home. She changed into her sweatpants and a flannel shirt. On cool days like this she wished they'd gone ahead and built the fireplace they'd talked about when they'd first moved in. Mike brought her a cup of tea, and Ludwig jumped up on the sofa next to her. She was about to lie down and pull up the comforter when her phone rang.

"Hello. Yes, I remember you—Maggie Stirling's neighbor. Really?" She grabbed the remote and turned to one of the afternoon talk shows. "Yes, he's talking to some reporter who wrote some book. School lunches?" She turned up the volume. The author was saying something about pesticides making school children sick. She held up her book, which each member of the studio audience was getting to take home.

Mike whispered, "What's going on?"

Susan continued her conversation with the neighbor. "You saw her at Maggie's? How can you possibly be sure it's the same woman after all these years? Okay, thanks for contacting me. I'll tell my daughter and the police will follow up."

"What was that all about?"

"Maggie's neighbor says the author on the talk show is the woman she saw at Maggie's several times thirty years ago."

"How can she be so sure?"

"The hair. The cute, swingy haircut she's sporting is the same one from back then."

"Every other woman had that haircut back then. It was a fad."

"But look at the skunk stripe on the side. That makes it unique. The neighbor says that's what makes her certain it's the same person."

The host of the talk show announced that the book was now available in bookstores.

"Mike, we have a Barnes & Noble in town. What do you say we go for a ride?" She changed into street clothes, ran a brush through her hair, and grabbed her purse. The bookstore was downtown next to Susan's favorite jewelry store. When they walked in, they immediately saw the book they were looking for staring at them from a display of recent best sellers in front of the entrance.

Sick to Their Stomachs—The Truth Behind School Lunches by Cynthia Thomas. "This is it." Susan flipped open the book. "Her bio says she was a reporter here in town during the seventies and eighties."

Mike grabbed a copy and flipped through the front. "Look at this list of books. She published an *exposé* on airline safety, one on toxic antibiotics, and another on veterinary fraud."

"*Exposés*. Did she happen to write one about contaminated water causing cancer in a local housing development?"

"I don't see one."

"Why not? She was working here in town during the scandal. It makes sense she would have been attracted to the story. Let's pop over to the library before it closes."

The public library was only two streets away. With help from the reference librarian, they scrolled through more microfiche.

"Look, Mike. Here it is. An article about the contaminated water in Tom Crow's housing development." Soon she found another article by the same reporter hinting that the builder knew about the contaminated water before he started building. "We have to get in touch with the author. I'll bet she was visiting Maggie to discuss the situation."

"Only which side was Maggie on? Was the reporter accusing her of being involved too?"

"I'm glad we bought a copy of the book before leaving the bookstore. I'll bet there's some sort of contact information."

Once in the car, Susan took the book out of the bag. "She lives in Vermont on a farm."

"Vermont's a small state, but still…"

"Here's an e-mail address. It says 'Contact the author.' I'll do just that."

Chapter 26

Two days had passed and the author/reporter still hadn't answered Susan's e-mail. Jonathan and Audrey had made a fruitless visit to Frank Paglieri, the disgruntled parent, after Susan told them about the reporter. *If I were that reporter, the first person I'd have talked to would have been a vocal parent whose child had been affected.* Lynette hadn't been able to verify Paglieri's alibi for the night the builder jumped (or was pushed) off the bridge. *If Lynette or Evan died because of an amoral builder and an eager real estate agent, I can see being angry enough to want to kill them. I wouldn't blame him if he murdered them both after the court found them innocent. The thing I wonder is if Maggie was in on it. Did she know about the contaminated water and ignore it, or was she just blissfully doing her job, naïve to the toxic drinking water?*

Susan arrived at Westbrook High earlier than usual so she could drop by Anna Cabrini's office and pump her for more information regarding her father, the builder, and Paglieri, the parent. Perhaps she'd seen the two of them together or knew that her father had received threats from him. The guidance office was much quieter than it had been the last time she'd dropped by.

"Hi, Mrs. Wiles. What can I do for you?"

"Anna, we've been investigating Frank Paglieri in relation to the Maggie Stirling case, but I was wondering if you could provide any more information about the relationship between Paglieri and your father. Your mother, when she was alive, swore your father would never have killed himself. If your father was in fact pushed off the bridge, Paglieri is the logical culprit."

Anna looked away. "I'm not comfortable talking about this."

"Anna, if Paglieri killed your father, he should pay. If you know anything, you have to tell the police."

"I can't." A tear streamed down Anna's cheek.

"Anna, focus. Did you ever hear the two men fighting? Did your dad receive phone calls or threats?"

"Stop! Just stop." Anna wiped her eyes. "Paglieri didn't kill my father."

"How can you be so sure? Do you know who did?"

"Why do you have to keep pushing me?"

"Anna…"

"Paglieri didn't kill my father. No one did. My father jumped off that bridge. He took his own life."

A student walked into the office. Anna hurriedly wiped her tears once again and took a deep breath before answering the student's question. As soon as he left, she continued.

"After my mother died, I sorted through her things, and I found a letter my father had written her. It was a suicide note. He said he was sorry for what he'd done to those children and their parents. He said even though the justice system hadn't convicted him, he knew he was guilty and couldn't live with the burden."

"Why did you keep it a secret?"

"What good would it have done? I didn't want my father's reputation to be further tarnished with his cowardice. It didn't matter at that point. The trial was long over."

Paglieri didn't kill the builder after all, but did he seek revenge on Maggie? "Anna, thanks for sharing that information as hard as it was. No one needs to know outside of the police. Now they can put their suspicions to rest. Your father killed himself; it wasn't a murder. Case closed."

Before going to the media center, Susan called Lynette and told her what she'd just learned.

"Mom, that's good to know. By the way, Paglieri didn't kill Axel either. He doesn't own a gun, and he's left-handed. The shot was made by someone right-handed."

"What about Maggie? He isn't off the hook for that yet. Did you verify an alibi?"

"We got DNA results back from the lab. There was DNA on the glove, but it wasn't Paglieri's. I should have known. Paglieri is thin and small boned. The glove even looked too big to be his. I'm glad Paglieri agreed to a cheek swab. Now he's officially in the clear."

"If the DNA wasn't Paglieri's, then whose was it?"

"We ran it through our databases and didn't get a match. Here's the kicker. It wasn't Richard Stirling's DNA either. There was an outsider in the house."

"The reporter! The neighbor and Axel both saw her at Maggie's on several occasions."

"Nope. The DNA came from a man. That much we know."

"Then what about the stalker? The one who sent her flowers?"

"We're still working on it. At the moment it's our only lead."

Richard is innocent after all? Impossible, Susan thought. *The schmuck was a womanizer, strung Audrey along all these years, got her to pay for teams of lawyers to the point she was ready to sell her house… and he's innocent?* She felt sick to her stomach. Then she remembered they still hadn't figured out who killed

Axel Schumaker. Even if they found the stalker and found him guilty of Maggie's murder, he had no connection to Axel Schumaker. Wait a minute… Unless the man who killed Maggie thought Axel *saw* him kill her!

Ginny, Maggie's good friend, had said to Susan that Maggie suspected the stalker was the guy who delivered supplies to her real estate office. And Maggie had a partner. Susan wondered if he was he still around. She walked into the media center where Janet greeted her warmly.

"Janet, I was wondering if you have any idea who Maggie's partner at the real estate office was. If I can track him down, maybe I'll learn more."

"Real estate office… wait. Let's check out the yearbooks from that time. The kids sell tons of ads every year. Most all local businesses contribute. It's good publicity." Janet went to a shelf and pulled out some bound yearbooks. "This is from the same year." She flipped to the back of the book.

"Wow, there are tons of ads," said Susan. "Looks like every business in town contributed."

"And neighboring towns. Here's a real estate ad. Ramos Realty. It lists Maggie's name and a Jefferson Ramos. Eureka. He must have been the partner you're looking for."

"Janet, you're incredible."

"I'd make a good Watson to your Sherlock. I *am* retiring next year."

"I'll keep it in mind. Scrapbooking and knitting really aren't all they're cracked up to be."

"Let's check public records on my office computer and see if we can get an address."

Susan's heart thumped with the adrenaline rush of a new clue. Janet knew her way around research and within minutes found Jefferson Ramos.

"Here you go, Susan. He owns his own real estate company. And it's right here in town. How lucky can you get?"

"You're amazing. I'm heading there as soon as I'm done here."

"Go on. You can stay longer next time. I want to hear about it after you meet him."

Susan couldn't believe her good fortune and admonished herself for not thinking of this earlier. She jumped in her newly repaired Prius and drove across town to Ramos Realty. It was right next door to her favorite bakery. Maybe afterward she'd duck in for an éclair.

Jefferson Ramos was a handsome middle-aged man with mud-colored eyes. She waited while he finished with a client, taking in the antique desk and Victorian-style chairs. A tasteful copy of a Rembrandt hung on the wall.

"What can I help you with? Large colonial to accommodate a brood of grandchildren? Condo love nest for you and your hubby?"

"Got a bachelorette pad big enough for a king-sized waterbed?"

Jefferson Ramos laughed and invited her to take a seat. Susan asked him about his former partner.

"Maggie Stirling. Lovely woman and my mentor. I was shocked to hear of her murder. That no-good husband did it to her."

Susan informed him that Richard might not be the guilty party after all. "I was wondering about the fires in the properties your office sold and about the one in your own office. Do you think it was arson?"

"I'm sure it was. Matt Caldwell. Shrewd businessman. Those properties were worthless until they burned down."

"You're saying he torched them?"

"No, not him. He was riddled with arthritis, could barely walk. I'm sure he paid someone to do the job. Maggie thought so too. Found a real pro. As much as they investigated, in each case it appeared to be an electrical fire. The thug knew what he was doing."

"Did Maggie find out who it was, or did she confront Matt Caldwell as far as you know?"

"She had her suspicions, but she didn't share them with me. Maggie was the type who'd never accuse someone without proof. I doubt she confronted Caldwell. She was after the hired hand." Jefferson Ramos offered her a cup of coffee and took a brief phone call.

"Your office, was it burned down as a threat?"

"Maggie was sure of it. Told me she knew who did it but needed evidence before going to the police."

"Do you think this thug knew she was on to him, and he killed her?"

Jefferson fingered his beard. "I hadn't thought about it. Maggie came in upset, even bruised, so many times I was convinced Richard killed her."

"There was one more thing I wanted to ask you about. Maggie's friend Ginny, as well as several others, told me Maggie was being stalked. Ginny said Maggie suspected the guy who delivered office supplies. Do you know what ever happened to him?"

"Far as I know he still lives with his parents. He was a little different, but stalking? Maybe... But killing, I can't imagine. His name is Darren. Darren Kent."

"Thank you so much for your time." Susan got back into the car and used her phone to search for Darren Kent's address. Before she'd finished, Brooks called her.

"Hi, Susan. I was checking on where things stand."

"I just found Maggie's real estate partner. I asked what he thought about the office burning down before

Maggie died. He told me he suspected a man named Matt Caldwell—'a shrewd businessman' as he put it."

"Say no more. I'm on it."

"Great. Meanwhile, Jefferson Ramos also gave me the name of the guy who used to deliver office supplies. According to her good friend, Maggie suspected him of being the stalker. I'm heading to find him now."

"I hadn't thought of him in years. I don't even remember his name."

"I got it from Jefferson. It's Darren Kent. I'll touch base with you later."

Susan found the address. Darren Kent lived down the road from the real estate office in a working-class community of modest houses. There were older model cars, trucks, and even a trailer or two in the driveways she passed. She had no idea what she'd say if his parents answered the door. As a matter of fact, she doubted either Darren or his parents would appreciate her implying that Darren had stalked and killed Maggie. *Come on, Susan. Think.*

While she sat parked in front of Darren Kent's house, thinking of a plausible story, the front door flew open. Out walked a middle-aged man wearing a McDonald's uniform. *How many middle-aged men live with their parents and work at McDonald's?* The man got into the ancient Dodge Dart sitting in his driveway. She decided to follow him.

Traffic was light, and Susan worried that Darren Kent would notice her tailing him, even though she kept as much distance between them as possible. Fortunately he showed no awareness. *Dang, I'm stuck at the light.* She drummed her fingers on the steering wheel as she watched him zip ahead. *Now what? I'm sure I lost him.*

Luckily, the light turned green within moments. She sped ahead and caught sight of the Dart just as it made a left turn. Soon the golden arches were visible. She pulled into the parking lot behind Darren Kent and sat in the car while she watched him go inside. *I can always go for French fries. I'll give him a few minutes to settle into his shift.*

She went inside and smelled the greasy fast food. She knew she should be repulsed by it, but instead her mouth began watering for fries. *What would Dr. Oz say to this?*

Darren took his place at the middle register. Susan got in his line.

"Welcome to McDonald's. Can I help you?" He spoke in a flat monotone.

Darren's eyes were steel blue and vacant. Susan shuddered when she looked at him. He didn't really look at her when he spoke; it was more like he was looking right through her. When he brought her the fries, Susan made her move.

"I'm going to be moving into town soon. I'm trying to find a place to live, but I barely know where to start. Can you recommend a real estate agent, or maybe point me in the right direction?"

"Do you want a hot apple pie with that?"

"No, thanks. Again, can you help me? Years and years ago, my friend—deceased now bless her soul—moved here. Bought a house from a Maggie Stirling." She whispered. "I heard the agent was murdered by her husband."

Darren began to repeatedly pound on the metal counter. He didn't speak but looked like a teakettle ready to boil its lid off. She noticed him taking deep breaths. Then he began counting slowly. Susan froze. Should she run away? As weird as his behavior was, she didn't feel as though she were in danger. Darren was still counting.

"Forty-one, forty-two, forty-three…"

The few customers in the restaurant looked at him, then continued eating. The manager came over and put his arm on Darren's shoulder."

"Don't touch me! Forty-four, forty-five, forty-six..."

The manager spoke in a soft voice and hugged him tightly around the shoulders. "Come on, Darren, let's go outside for a few minutes. It's going to be okay."

While the manager went outside with Darren, the cashier at the next register spoke to her.

"Darren is a pussycat and a hard worker. Don't let his behavior scare you. He's on *the spectrum.* You know, like *Rain Man.* Sometimes he gets set off like that. Most of the time he's fine. The manager knows how to handle him."

"Thanks," said Susan. She grabbed her fries and left. I can't imagine him plotting a murder. Maybe I'll go back to his house and see if his parents can tell me anything. She drove back to the Kent residence.

Mrs. Kent invited Susan to come in. Susan explained she was looking for suspects in the Maggie Stirling murder.

"I met Darren," Susan said. "I know he didn't kill Maggie, but since he delivered supplies to her office, I thought he may have seen things. Maggie had a stalker. Did he ever mention anything like that to you?"

"Goodness, thirty years ago? I know Darren had a crush on her. He sent her flowers once. I told him he shouldn't do that. He has some trouble with social skills. He was upset when he learned she was killed."

"Did he find out right away? Did someone at her office tell him?"

"No, he found out later. We went to visit my parents over the holidays. When we got back to town, it was all over the news about Maggie Stirling's murder. They say her husband did it. Last I heard, he's in jail."

"So you and Darren were out of town when Maggie was killed. Where do your parents live?"

"Lived. They've been gone some time now, but they lived in Arizona."

Darren wasn't even in town when Maggie was murdered. He may or may not have been her stalker, but he wasn't her killer. Susan noted that this was another dead end.

Chapter 27

The next morning Susan drove to the hotel, where Jonathan, Audrey, and Brooks were eating breakfast. She filled them in on what she'd learned.

"The DNA wasn't a match to Richard, but it definitely came from a man. I checked out the guy who delivered office supplies to Maggie. He did have a crush on her, but he's autistic and didn't seem capable of plotting a murder and covering his tracks. Besides, he has an alibi. He was in Arizona visiting his grandparents at the time of the murder."

"So it wasn't the stalker," said Brooks.

Audrey stood up. "See, I told you Richard was innocent. I knew the DNA wouldn't match."

Brooks said, "I hope that's enough to get a new trial. They may say Richard was wearing a different pair of gloves and the glove was left by someone not involved in the murder. Maybe it belonged to Maggie herself."

"Whose side are you on?" said Audrey. "Don't you want Richard to get a new trial? I thought you were his friend."

"Of course I'm his friend. I'm trying to think of every angle. Assuming Richard gets a new trial, you know how it goes. The lawyer with the best creative flair wins. I just want to make sure our side is airtight."

"I think it's time to visit Richard. Surely the jail is accepting visitors by now," said Susan. "Jonathan, will you come with me?"

"I don't think they caught the escapees yet," said Brooks.

"Surely they have." Jonathan stood up and paced in a circle. "I haven't seen Richard in so many years." He paced a bit longer. After a few minutes he answered, "Sure. Let's go. I have to go up to my room first to get my jacket."

"I want to go with you too," whined Audrey.

"The jail won't allow three of us in at once," said Jonathan. "Go with Brooks and work on trying to talk to the reporter since she hasn't responded to Susan's e-mail. Come on, Susan. Let's go."

Audrey opened her mouth to object, but Brooks led her away. Jonathan pushed the elevator button. It was midmorning and the lobby was empty.

"It'll take about an hour to get to the prison," said Susan. "I'm hoping we can learn something from your brother to point us in the right direction. Do you think it's enough that Richard's DNA isn't on the glove?"

"I don't know," replied Jonathan pressing the button for his floor. "The glove was mishandled, so it may be excluded. If we could prove someone else murdered Maggie, it would be more convincing. All these years I thought it was Richard. If it isn't, the real killer should pay. We owe it to Maggie to do what we can."

All of a sudden the elevator shook, and there was a loud bang. The lights flicked off. Susan's heart skipped a beat. "Jonathan, what's happening?" Like an aftershock from an earthquake, the elevator shook once again. Susan grabbed Jonathan's arm. "What's going on?"

"Must have been a power shortage. I'm sure the backup generator will kick in. We'll be moving soon."

Susan took a few deep breaths and tried to calm down. *Jonathan's voice is so reassuring. It's a shame he didn't get the chance to be a father,* she thought. Her claustrophobia was rearing its ugly head. *The power will come on in a minute. I will not panic, I will not panic... Focus on something else.*

"Jonathan, do you think you and Richard will have a relationship if he's in fact innocent?"

"I'm not sure. It's hard not having any family, but after believing Richard was guilty all these years, it will take some work. I don't know where he'll settle down if he does get out. He has no ties and will need a job."

"I'm sure Audrey's hoping he'll move to Florida. As a matter of fact, he might do just that. After all, it would be a free place to stay, meals, Audrey doting over him like he's a God..."

Jonathan chuckled.

"I can see it now," said Susan. "Audrey will go off to the school, and Richard will stay in bed till noon."

"Then he'll go into the kitchen and heat up whatever Audrey made him for breakfast, linger over the newspaper, do the crossword puzzle... Always got his way when we were growing up. I shoveled snow, he sat inside and baked cookies with our mom."

"Speaking of brothers, if that happens, Audrey's son George won't be happy. He works for the DEA down in Florida. Has a detective's instincts. He thought Richard was big-time trouble for Audrey."

The elevator shook, then the emergency lights went out. It was pitch dark. Susan groped along the walls until she found the door and started banging. "Help! We're trapped in here." She felt a panic attack starting. He throat was tight, and her heart beat faster.

"Don't worry, they'll find us soon." Jonathan put his arm around Susan. "Here, let's sit down while we wait."

Susan groped for her phone. "There's no service. I should have known. Isn't there an emergency phone in here?"

"Yes, but the cord's been cut. I noticed it right away."

Susan took a deep breath. "I can't believe they haven't found us yet."

"Perhaps the entire hotel has no electricity. It won't be long. Tell me about your children. How did your daughter get into detective work?"

"Lynette always wanted to be a detective. She gobbled up Nancy Drew books when she was younger. I'm glad I'd saved my collection. She went into the police academy right after college."

"And you have a granddaughter, right?"

"Annalise. Beautiful girl, smart too. Lynette and Jason tried a long time to have her. Thank God she's here."

"Infertility is a tough road. My wife and I rode that roller coaster for many years. I'm still sorry we didn't try adoption." The lights blinked on momentarily, then back off.

Susan and Jonathan took turns telling their life stories. Then they talked about philosophies, hobbies, books, politics… Jonathan had a candy bar from the vending machine in his pocket and shared the partially melted chocolate with his daughter.

Susan felt hot and shaky. She didn't know how much longer she could stand being stuck inside this tomb. "Jonathan, it's been hours. What if we run out of air?"

"These things aren't airtight. We'll be okay. In fact, do you hear something?"

Susan listened against the door. "Yes, I hear something. Sounds like grinding."

Suddenly, the lights came back, and seconds later, two maintenance workers opened the door. Susan threw her arms around one of them. "Thank God you found us."

"Power's been out. We had to track down the problem. Never have trouble with the electricity here— not unless there's a storm. We found a frayed wire finally. Odd."

"Thanks for getting us out. Jonathan, do you still want to go to the prison?"

"It's late. Let's go in the morning. Besides, we've had enough stress for the day."

With flight or fight taunting her body all morning, she hadn't realized she was starving, in spite of the half-melted Hershey's bar that Jonathan had shared with her. The first thing she did when she got home was make a late lunch. Grilled cheese and tomato soup. Comfort food at its best. Both Johann and Ludwig came running when they smelled the cheese. Susan's phone rang.

"Hi, Lynette. What a morning." Susan told Lynette about her elevator adventure.

"Mom, I found information about the stalker, the one who sent Maggie flowers. He was arrested on a similar case the next town over before Maggie's murder. He's not our killer."

"I hope Richard Stirling can offer some help. Jonathan and I are going to the prison tomorrow. I'll call you afterward."

Susan had barely hung up with Lynette when the phone rang again. It was Audrey.

I knew she'd be pumping me about information about Richard. She'll have to wait a little longer, Susan thought.

Susan relayed the day's events to her birth mother.

Audrey said, "Today was a total waste. You didn't get to see Jonathan, and Brooks took me on a wild-goose chase. First he sends me ahead to the public library in a cab—no less—to get started while he "took care of some business." Then when he finally gets there, we spin our wheels trying to find information. If you're going to the prison tomorrow, please let me tag along. We can take turns visiting Richard if they won't let us in at one time."

"Audrey, I don't think it's a good idea."

Audrey whined and pleaded until Susan broke down and agreed to take her along. She couldn't help thinking, *me and my parents going to visit my... uncle. Yuck, I hadn't thought of Richard as my uncle until now. This is going to be interesting.*

Chapter 28

The next morning Susan swung by the hotel to pick up Jonathan and Audrey. She suggested Jonathan sit in the front, with his long legs and all. Audrey's chatter annoyed her—even from the backseat. The sky was clear, and the sun streamed strongly through the windshield.

"I can't wait to see Richard. He must be so happy that he'll be coming home soon," said Audrey. Susan rolled her eyes. Audrey had put on a dress and red lipstick for the occasion.

"Remember these things aren't always quick," said Jonathan. "Even if we get an evidentiary hearing and are granted a new trial, it could be another year before he gets out. Providing he's found innocent."

Susan looked in the rearview mirror. "That car's been behind me the whole time. He's following right on my tail."

"Maybe he's visiting the prison too," said Audrey.

Sure, Susan thought, *doesn't everyone have a boyfriend/brother/uncle/ in prison?*

The car swerved around the driver's side and peeled ahead.

"He's in a hurry," said Audrey.

Blinded by the sun, Susan couldn't see the car that had just pulled ahead of her. She reached for her sunglasses, but they didn't help much. "Just as well he passed me. I don't like being tailed."

"We're getting close. I can't wait to see Richard. He'll…"

Suddenly the other car whipped around in the middle of the highway and slammed into the back of Susan's car with such force that Audrey was knocked unconscious. Susan hit her chest against the steering wheel. Thank God she was wearing her seat belt and the airbag inflated. Still she felt as if her ribs were bruised or even broken. Her glasses were bent.

"Susan, are you okay?" Jonathan had the red beginnings of a black eye from the impact of his airbag. He managed to unbuckle his seat belt and with wobbly legs, got out, walked around the mangled car, and with difficulty, opened Susan's door. "Here, can you walk?"

Susan grabbed Jonathan's arm and got out. "My ribs hurt, and I feel shaky. How did that car hit us from behind? It passed me."

"Was it the same car?"

"Yes, I think so. Is Audrey okay? Audrey!" Susan pulled the back door handle. "I can't open it."

Jonathan grabbed it and pulled. "Here we go, it's open. She's unconscious. Call 911. We shouldn't move her."

Susan called 911, then Lynette and Mike. She began to wobble. Jonathan grabbed her.

"Come on, let me help you sit back down." She sat on a small patch of grass beside the road and tried to bend her bifocals enough to get them on her nose. She heard sirens approaching.

The paramedics went immediately to Audrey. They carefully extracted her from the car and, keeping her immobile, lifted her onto a stretcher. She still hadn't regained consciousness.

One of the paramedics came to Susan, strapped on a blood-pressure cuff, and examined her ribs. "You may have a break." He helped her into the ambulance beside Audrey.

"I'll wait here for the police," said Jonathan.

"We can't leave you here." The paramedic checked him over. As he was doing it, a police car pulled up. Lynette and Jackson hopped out.

"Mom, are you okay? What happened? What's wrong with Audrey?"

"A car deliberately rammed into the side of my Prius. It had been tailing me for a while. Audrey is unconscious."

The paramedic said, "We need to take them to the hospital *asap*." He motioned to Jonathan.

"Can I stay here with the police? I can give them a description of what happened."

Lynette looked at her grandfather tenderly, thankful he hadn't been badly hurt. She wanted to have the chance to spend time with him and get to know him. "It's okay. I'll take him with me."

Both on stretchers, Susan held Audrey's hand all the way to the hospital. Life and death situations had a funny way of putting things in perspective. Suddenly, Audrey was a vulnerable old lady who might never wake up, rather than the lying monster Susan had been seeing her as. *She's so pale, and her hand is so cold.*

"Ma'am, let me bandage those ribs. At the hospital they'll take X-rays, but if anything's broken, we don't want them moving around."

"Don't worry. It hurts too much to move."

At the hospital, Susan was whisked into X-ray. By the time they got her to a bed in the treatment area, Mike was waiting.

"Are you okay? By the time I got to where you had the accident you were already gone."

"I'm okay. Maybe some broken ribs." She flinched as she reached for his hand. "Do you know anything about Audrey's condition?"

"They're still running tests. They released Jonathan. Looks like he's going to have quite a shiner, but he's fine other than that."

The doctor came in with Susan's test results. "Nothing's broken, but those ribs may hurt for a while. Soft tissues are traumatized in an injury like you suffered. Take Tylenol for the pain, and take it easy. No lifting. Check with your regular doctor in a few weeks."

While Mike filled out paperwork and insurance information, Susan asked if she could see Audrey. The nurse told her Audrey was awake and brought her to the room.

Audrey's hair was matted with dried blood over the stitches on her forehead. "Audrey, are you okay? We were worried about you."

"I have the worst headache ever. I have to stay overnight for observation, but the tests show nothing serious. Possibly a concussion."

Now I feel like a real heel being so mad at her and treating her so badly. She could have died, thought Susan.

"Audrey, I'm sorry for being so angry. It's just been hard, digesting one secret after another. First I find out I'm adopted, then I'm told you never saw my father again, then I find out you were lying to me, and Jonathan is my birth father. Now I'm not supposed to tell Jonathan he's my father. Oh, and my Uncle Richard is in jail for murdering his wife... maybe. It's a lot for an old lady to handle."

"I'm the one who's sorry. I was so young when I had you—barely fifteen years old. I didn't want Jonathan to give up his dream of going to law school, especially since I knew my parents would never let me keep you. When you came into my life, I hadn't seen Jonathan in decades and I couldn't bring myself to tell him I'd kept you from him."

"After this is over, I'm going to tell him. I want him to be part of my life, and I want Lynette and Evan to know him."

"I understand. Before I met you, the only family I had was my son, George. It was wonderful realizing I also had you, grandchildren—even a great granddaughter. I can understand how important that would be to Jonathan."

"That's right. Now that he's a widow, he has no family... except Richard. Who knows if he can ever make peace with him after all these years even if Richard turns out to be innocent?"

"He *is* innocent. Richard is definitely innocent."

The door opened, and Lynette came in with Mike. Mike handed Audrey a *get well soon* balloon bouquet he'd gotten at the gift shop. Lynette pulled a notepad from her purse.

"Audrey, it's good to see you awake and alert. Now, can either of you remember anything at all about the car that hit you?"

"The sun was in my eyes," said Susan. "It was dark, black, I think. A biggish sedan. Nothing that set it apart."

"Yes, Susan. That's what I saw too. And I remember a few numbers from the tag."

Three pair of eyes focused on Audrey as she recited some numbers. *She probably has a concussion, and she actually remembers some numbers off the license plate? That's my mother,* thought Susan.

Lynette said, "Sounds like a rental. I'll put out a description and check with the local agencies."

"I'll swing by tomorrow and take you back to the hotel," said Mike. "I took Jonathan back earlier."

Susan swallowed hard. "You can stay with us for a few days. Just to make sure you're okay." *I hope I won't regret making that offer.*

"Thank you, Susan. I'd love that. Hey, I just thought of something. Where's Brooks? Did anyone tell him what happened?"

Mike said, "I stopped by his room when I dropped off Jonathan, but he wasn't there. Front desk said they hadn't seen him all day."

"I'll call him. Rest up. You've had a tough day."

Mike stopped for Chinese takeout on the way home. Susan was starving as well as exhausted. She craved curling up on the sofa with the remote and her cats. After dinner she checked her phone messages.

"Mike, I got a message from Emily. She and Henry are retiring and moving to Vermont!"

"Really? Aren't they a little young to quit working?"

"I'll get the scoop tomorrow. Emily wants to meet for lunch. Henry's been a successful doctor all these years, and they don't have kids. I doubt money is an issue. Why not enjoy the second half of their lives?" She patted Mike on the shoulder. Although he had cut back on his work hours after his heart attack, she looked forward to the day he fully retired. Perhaps they could be snowbirds and live in Florida during the winters.

Susan looked forward to seeing her oldest and dearest friend. The next day she put on her newest jeans and a colorful blouse. Emily was waiting for her when she arrived at Vinny's.

"Susan, so glad you could make it on short notice," said Emily. Emily also wore jeans, which she paired with a cream cable-knit sweater. She was eight years Susan's junior.

"My schedule's pretty flexible these days," said Susan. "While I used to fit in a full-time job in addition to a slew of other chores without batting an eye, now it takes me all day to choose a time to run to ShopRite. And then I need a nap! Getting old is no fun."

Emily laughed. "I'll never picture you as old. And I'm looking forward to retirement myself."

"I heard on your message. I thought you and Henry planned to work another ten years."

"We did. But Henry's mother died, leaving us the place in Vermont. We considered selling it, but it holds so many memories of growing up. After a short discussion we decided to keep it and move up there. We already have a buyer for our place here in Westbrook."

"Vermont will be a great place for you two."

"I know, that's what we thought. We both love hiking, rowing, cross-country skiing... Why not enjoy what we love while we're still young enough to get around? Besides, I can write from anywhere, and I saw an ad that the local college is looking for part-time instructors. Maybe I'll be able to teach a journalism class. Henry can work from there too. He can read radiology reports from his computer and not have the stress of being full time with the hospital."

A waitress wearing the colors of the Italian flag handed them menus and brought drinks. The lunch crowd was beginning to filter in. Vinny's had delicious and affordable lunch specials. Susan ordered a slice of pizza with minestrone soup. Emily got the meatball sub with salad.

"You and Mike will have to come visit."

"I'd love to. Do you think you'll miss working for the newspaper?"

"I've worked for the *Westbrook Post* my whole career. I'm looking forward to having time to write books. I already have plenty of ideas based on what I've seen as a reporter."

"So you're going to specialize in true crime?"

"I don't know about specialize, but it's a starting point."

"Speaking of reporters, do you by any chance remember a reporter named Cynthia Thomas?"

"Yes, I sure do. She was already working for the paper when I was hired. She was their top dog. That woman knew how to get a story. She wasn't past crawling in people's backyards, digging through trash cans, doing her own personal stakeouts… She got some great stories, I've got to admit."

"Would she have been likely to peek into windows or pressure a source?"

"Yes, I'd say so. She's a successful author now. I've read a few of her books. She does *exposés*."

The waitress brought the soup and salad. The restaurant was virtually full now.

"I'm surprised she didn't write about the contaminated water scandal."

"She was working on something, then dropped it and took a better job in the city."

"Emily, I'm going to miss you and Henry."

"Let's schedule a visit right now. How about end of February? Snow should be good then, and we can go cross-country skiing."

"I'm not promising you'll catch me on a pair of skis, but we'd love to visit. February it is."

The next morning, Susan checked her e-mail before breakfast.

"Mike, I heard back from that author/reporter Cynthia Thomas. She says she's going to be in town tomorrow and asked if we can meet at Barnes & Noble. She says she has information, but she feels more comfortable sharing it in person."

"As long as you're feeling up to it, go ahead. We have the rental. Hopefully you'll get the Prius back soon. Do you think you can drive? The doctor said to be careful with your ribs."

"I'll be fine. According to Emily, this Cynthia was quite a character. Would do just about anything for a story. I can't wait to hear what she has to say."

Chapter 29

Barnes & Noble was one of Susan's favorite places in the world. She'd spent countless hours browsing the shelves and reading, especially right after she retired. Today, she arrived a little early and flipped through the new releases while waiting for Cynthia Thomas to arrive. When the reporter walked into the store right on time, Susan had no trouble recognizing her from the author photo on the back of her new book.

"Hello, you must be Cynthia Thomas. I'm Susan Wiles."

Cynthia was dressed in tailored tweed pants and a cream sweater. Her nails sported a perfect French manicure. From her hands and the subtle lines around her eyes, Susan guessed they were about the same age. The reporter followed Susan into the café section, and they ordered coffee before sitting near the railing overlooking the floor.

"When I read your e-mail, I felt compelled to speak to you. I was close to Maggie Stirling and surprised at hearing that her husband may be getting a new trial. After all these years? I figured there must be a good story behind it."

"You don't know the half of it. Somehow I've managed to be part of a team looking into other suspects who may have killed Maggie. One of her neighbors recognized you recently when she saw you on a talk show. There were reports from her and Maggie's next-door neighbor that you were at

Maggie's, sometimes late at night. One witness reported seeing your red sports car in her driveway."

"You mean my green sports car. I drove a sage-colored Miata back then. Maggie was helping me with a story. I was putting together an *exposé* on the contaminated drinking water. I was sure the company down the road from the development and the builder, Tom Crow, knew about the health hazard and covered it up."

"Did you think Maggie was part of the cover-up?"

"I *know* she wasn't. Not willingly at least. The company was paying off both her and the builder to keep them quiet. Tom Crow played both sides. He didn't have a problem taking hush money, though the profits he made were incentive enough not to come forward."

"Maggie received regular deposits into her bank account. Was that from the company?"

"Yes. We documented all the deposits made into her account so I could use it in my story. Maggie was determined to stop the cover-up once she heard about those children dying of cancer."

So Maggie was a white hat. She was working with Cynthia to make things right. What about the angry parents? Did Cynthia interview them? Susan had so many questions.

"Did you ever speak to a man named Paglieri? His son died of cancer, and he was quite vocal about the situation. We wondered if he blamed Maggie for selling him the house in the first place. It crossed our minds he may have killed her."

"Paglieri? A killer?" scoffed Cynthia. "Heavens, no! He was working *with* me and Maggie on the story. We met many times, all three of us. He was grateful for Maggie's compassion and sense of duty. He didn't kill her."

As it got closer to lunch time, more shoppers filled the store, and the café went into overdrive serving croissant sandwiches, soups, and salads. Resisting the chocolate turnovers and cheesecake bars, Susan bought another round of coffee to justify taking up the seats.

When she returned, she said, "How come the story was never published? I saw some newspaper articles about the scandal, but nothing as detailed as you were working on. Why didn't you publish a book like you did on the other investigations you made?"

"Maggie was murdered. Then Tom Crow drowned in the Hudson River. I felt it was in poor taste to continue. I moved on and took a job writing a column for a leading paper in the city."

"Did you notice anything suspicious at all? Did Maggie mention being threatened? Was anyone else involved in writing the story?"

Cynthia sipped her coffee and took a few minutes to remember. "Not really. There was one time when the three of us met for lunch to work on the story... A blond, curly-haired guy came up to us. Said he had to talk to Maggie about something important. She brushed him off, and he stomped out of the restaurant like an angry child. After he left, Maggie made a comment about him being like a gnat that buzzed in your ear. It could have been anything."

"Thanks for meeting with me."

"Hope I helped. Can I do anything else for you?"

"One more thing."

"Sure."

Susan pulled Cynthia's new book out of her oversized purse. "Would you sign this for me?"

Chapter 30

All our suspects have been eliminated. If Richard didn't kill Maggie, who did? Whose DNA is on that glove? Third time's the charm. Today I'm going to get to that prison and meet with Richard Stirling. I'm sure he holds the key to solving the case, whether he realizes it or not, Susan thought.

Susan kissed Mike good-bye, handed him his lunch box, and continued eating her egg-white omelet, which was getting cold and tasting more like rubber cement by the minute. She dumped it in the trash and poured herself a bowl of Special K—the one chock-full of chocolate chunks.

Audrey, in her pink terry bathrobe, padded into the dining room with a cup of coffee. "Susan, I want to go with you and Jonathan to the prison today."

"I don't think it's a good idea. You should rest and be sure that head heals."

"I'm fine. I need to see Richard."

Susan's phone vibrated on the table. "Jonathan, I'll be there in half an hour. What? A conference call? Can't you tell them you're busy this morning?"

"What's wrong?" said Audrey.

Susan turned away from her, covering her free ear. "Okay. I'll let you know what happens."

Audrey grabbed her arm. "What happened? Isn't Jonathan going with you to the prison?"

"No, he's got a mandatory conference call with the law school. Guess I'm going alone." She remembered last time she went alone to the prison. An ear-piercing alarm had sounded, the doors had automatically locked, and she had been trapped in a room with a not-so-pleasant guard for hours.

"Then I'm certainly going with you," said Audrey. "I'll keep you company."

Go up by myself, though I'm still a bit gun-shy going solo, wait for Jonathan to be available another day, or go with Audrey? Susan asked herself. "Okay, Audrey. Get dressed and we'll take a ride."

Snow flurries fell on the windshield. Susan wasn't used to driving a big car anymore and was looking forward to ditching this rental and getting her Prius back. There was little traffic, and soon they climbed the two-lane road up the mountain, past the weathered sign that read *Bayersville State Correctional Facility.* Like last time, the sight of cement walls and the rusty barbed wire fence gave her the chills. She stared at the lookout tower and wondered who was asleep on the job the day those prisoners had escaped. Then she had a shuddering thought. *What if those escaped prisoners are hanging out nearby? They could be waiting to ambush and steal an escape vehicle.*

Audrey said, "I'm excited about seeing Richard. Does my hair look okay?"

"Your hair looks fine. I'd blot off some of that Hollywood Vamp red lipstick if I were you though. Don't make him think you're trying too hard." *Seriously, I can't believe she's trapped in Richard's web. If he does get out, I hope she'll see him for who he is and come to her senses.*

They entered a cinder block lobby with one small window next to the door. They rang the bell on the counter, and the receptionist slid open a frosted glass sliding window and had them sign in. She took their ID's and issued visitor's passes, which they stuck to their shirts, then they waited for a guard to escort them to the first security checkpoint. While they waited, Susan asked the receptionist when the prison had reopened for visitors.

The receptionist answered, "Reopened? We were only shut down for less than forty-eight hours."

All this time we could have been talking to Richard? Susan thought.

A dark, wavy-haired guard with a jelly belly opened the door. As soon as he saw her, he said, "Oh no, not you again!"

It was the same guard Susan had gotten trapped with the last time she'd visited. His belly had grown in the interim, stretching his uniform shirt tightly across his middle.

"Nice to see you too," said Susan. She and Audrey followed him through the security checkpoints. The halls were noisy and smelled vaguely like urine. They continued into the visitation room. Audrey's eyes lit up as soon as the jumpsuit-clad Richard took a seat on the other side of the partition. *He looks like an overgrown pumpkin. How can Audrey possibly be attracted to him?* Audrey was jumping out of her skin with excitement, so Susan let her talk first. Afterward, she took the phone and started asking questions.

"Richard, your DNA didn't match the DNA left on the glove."

"That's great news. It proves someone else was in the house that night. Do they know whose DNA it is?"

"No, and since the glove was mishandled as evidence, it's tainted. It may not be admissible. Can you think of anyone else who wanted to kill Maggie? How about her sister, Adair, or Adair's boyfriend, Chase?"

"No way, José. Maggie and Adair got along like two peas in a pod. They weren't speaking for a while, but after Adair got clean and sobered up, they made up. Maggie even sent her plane tickets to come visit. Chase was a good guy. Lived down the road from us. I got him a construction job down in Atlanta, then he moved back and decided to become a cop. We even helped him move his things from his parent's house to a rental nearer to the academy. Piled all his worldly goods into Brooks's red hippy van."

"Can you think of anyone else? Anyone who was mad at or had an ax to grind with her?"

"The only thing I can think of is this phone call she got one night. I came home from work and heard her yelling into the phone."

"What was she saying?"

"Something about 'How could you do that? Aare you crazy?' Then she told the caller she was going to head down to the police station in the morning."

"And did she? Did she go to the police station?"

"I don't know. She was killed the following night. I asked her who she was talking to, but she said it was nothing. Stormed upstairs and never answered me."

The guard held up five fingers, signaling they were about out of time. Susan tried to remember everything she wanted to ask him and was afraid she was forgetting something.

Richard said, "You know, Maggie's office burned down. I never connected the two incidents. The fire was ruled accidental, but there was talk of arson for a while. I don't know if it means anything."

"It might. I'll tell Jonathan. Lynette can look into it. We have nothing else to go on."

Richard blew Audrey a kiss. Then he said, "Tell Brooks I said *hi*. It was good seeing him the other day."

The other day? Brooks never mentioned visiting Richard. In fact, he'd insisted the prison was on lockdown. Susan was confused.

Richard was taken back to his cell. Susan and Audrey followed Guard Jelly Belly back through security to the prison entrance. Susan was happy to breathe the outside air. It was snowing harder than when they'd first arrived.

So, Susan thought as she drove through the snow silently. *Adair and Chase were on good terms with Maggie. Maggie argued on the phone with someone shortly before her murder. Her office burned down. Brooks lied about Adair and Chase... I came hoping for answers, but I'm leaving with a whole new set of questions.*

Chapter 31

Susan stopped by the police station to update Lynette before going home. Her ribs were aching, and Audrey was rubbing her head. Susan suggested Audrey stay in the car to rest, popped two aspirin herself, and made her way inside the unusually quiet station. Lynette was at her computer, catching up on paperwork.

"Lynette, there was a fire in Maggie's office. Richard said they thought it was arson. The investigation couldn't prove it was. Can you dig up some information?"

"If it wasn't deemed arson, there's no point. The office had to be insured. I'll check Maggie's financials and see if she deposited a check from the insurance company, but I don't remember any big deposits other than those I told you about."

"The fire happened not long before Maggie's murder. She wouldn't have gotten the money by then. The papers must have run articles on a suspicious fire. Let me see your computer."

"It was too long ago. There won't be information online. You'd need to dig through the newspapers at the library."

Susan heard the reception gate creak open. A moment later she gasped. Adair Porter walked into the office.

"Adair? I thought you were away. What are you doing in New York?"

"The woman at the counter said I could come back to talk to Detective Green. I was on a cruise, didn't even take my phone with me. As soon as I got home, I saw all kinds of messages and thought I'd fly up here while I had a few days of vacation left. What's going on? Did you find anything more on my sister's murder?"

Lynette stood up. "They found DNA on the glove, which wasn't a match for Richard. Our star witness, Axel Schumaker, was murdered. No one at the hotel heard or saw anything."

"Axel Schumaker, the boy who lived next door to Maggie? How was he killed? That's unreal. I guess Richard has a rock-solid alibi for that one."

"He was shot with a small-caliber gun. Had to have had a silencer. Someone doesn't want Richard to get off on Maggie's murder."

"Yeah," said Adair. "Probably Maggie's real murderer. He's been running around free all these years…"

Susan added, "We had three possible suspects for Axel's murder—Paglieri, the angry parent whose son died of cancer, a mysterious dark-haired woman with a Dorothy Hamill haircut, and a stalker who'd sent Maggie flowers and spray-painted her front when she didn't return his feelings."

Adair collapsed into one of the chairs. Lynette brought her some water. She took a few deep breaths. "Where do you stand with them?"

Lynette said, "We found out the woman—Cynthia Thomas—was a reporter. She, Paglieri, and Maggie were working together to bring down the company that knowingly dumped hazardous waste into the water supply. The reporter-turned-author specializes in writing *exposés*."

Lynette's partner, Jackson Simpson, poked his head in the office. Ever since he'd found out he was going to be a father, Susan sensed a lightness, a sense of contentment. Marrying Theresa had been an incredibly positive influence on him, and the baby-to-be was already multiplying the effect. Where she and Jackson were once verbal sparring partners, he'd lost his edginess, and picking on him wasn't nearly as much fun lately.

"I got the official arrest report on Maggie's 'stalker.' He's out of prison now but has kept his nose clean ever since his release. Charley Kelly sent it right over."

"Charley Kelly?" said Adair. Her face flushed pink. "You mean my Charley Kelly? He's still in the area?"

"What do you mean? How do you know Sergeant Kelly?" said Lynette.

"Charley Kelly. *Chase* Kelly. When he decided to go to the academy, he didn't think Chase was a fitting name for an officer! He joked that he should call himself Catch'm Kelly instead. He settled on Charley." Adair's expression changed from anxious to dreamy. *Is she still carrying a torch for him after all these years? Chase was under our noses all this time!*

Jackson said, "He's alive and kicking. Not married either," and returned to his office.

Susan said, "You mentioned you were single. Why don't you drop by his station? It's the next town over."

Adair was silent then said, "Maybe I will…"

Jackson ran back into Lynette's office, flushed and speaking quickly. "It's Theresa! She's at the hospital."

Lynette said, "But it's too soon. What happened?"

"She was working in her classroom after school, and she started having contractions. The teacher next door to her luckily was there late too. She just called. She's with Theresa at the hospital. I have to get over there."

He fumbled through his pockets for his keys. "Where are my keys? Where did I put them?"

Lynette said, "They're in your desk drawer where you always keep them. I wish I could drive you over there, but we can't both leave."

Susan said, "I'll take you, Jackson. Come on! Audrey's in the car."

Jackson stumbled over his words as they headed out. "She's not due yet. We were just at the doctor yesterday. Everything was fine. He said everything looked good."

Audrey had been napping in the backseat. "What's wrong?"

"We're taking Jackson to the hospital. His wife is there." She flew through the icy streets like a pro and let Jackson off out front. "I'm going to park, and we'll be right there."

Susan calculated in her head. *She's due in about eight weeks. It will be okay. Even if she has the baby now, they will both be fine. Dear God, please watch over Theresa and her baby. Let them both be safe.*

When Susan and Audrey got to the labor and delivery floor, she immediately saw Jackson talking to a nurse. He looked like he was about to melt into a heap on the floor. Susan gave him a hug. "It's going to be okay."

"They're giving her something to try to stop the contractions. What if the baby dies? What if something happens to Theresa? I'm going back there now."

"Audrey and I will be right out here. If you need anything, just tell us." She and Audrey sat in the waiting room, which was more comfy and bright than most waiting rooms she'd been in. The walls were painted baby blue, with a mural of a stork flying over a forest with a bundle of babies in his beak. A vending machine stood in the corner.

"Do you want a soda?" said Susan.

Audrey dug change out of her coat pocket. "I'll get it. Two Diet Cokes coming up."

When Susan finally sat down with her drink and had a chance to breathe, she thought about the conversation she'd had with Richard at the prison and the surprise appearance of Adair at the station. *Why had Brooks lied about Adair and Chase?*

"Audrey, you and Brooks went to school together. Can you think of any reason he would have lied about Adair and Maggie reconciling? And about the prison being on lockdown?"

"Brooks always did like to take shortcuts. And he's always been spacey. I'll bet when he couldn't find Adair, he found it more convenient to make something up rather than admit he came up empty-handed. I'll bet he never even checked if Adair had been to New York."

"Why did he leave law school so abruptly, do you know?"

"He was struggling. I heard from Richard he was on academic probation. We thought he'd try to stick out the semester, but he left rather suddenly. Richard had just moved to New York, and I guess Brooks seized the opportunity to work up there."

Jackson came into the waiting room. "The medicine isn't working. She's having the baby tonight. They gave her something to help get the baby's lungs ready."

Susan walked over to the vending machine and returned with a bag of Cheetos. "I know Lynette hounds you about eating orange junk foods, but you deserve this."

Jackson tore open the bag. "Thanks, I haven't eaten all day. I'm going back in."

Susan called Mike and Lynette with the update.

"Audrey, let's run to the cafeteria and get some dinner. It's late. You must be hungry. I know I am."

The cafeteria smelled like beef stew. Three quarters of the tables were filled with hospital personnel clad in white coats, green scrubs, or colorful smocks. At other tables, diners ate alone with their phones or quietly with limited companionship.

Susan and Audrey grabbed trays, which they piled with soggy pot roast, mixed vegetables, and slices of carrot cake.

"Audrey, could Richard have set the girls' dorm on fire back at Tarrington? Answer from your head, not your lovesick heart."

"No, absolutely not. He couldn't even get a fire going for a barbecue in his own backyard. Believe me, I witnessed it with my own eyes. Besides, the fire in the dorm was accidental."

"There was accelerant on the glove at the crime scene. Then Richard told us Maggie's office burned down. I'm thinking there's a connection, but I don't know what, or should I say *who*, it is." She checked her phone. "Nothing from Jackson. Do you want to go home or stick around until the baby is born?"

"I had a nap in the car. Let's stay."

Susan and Audrey went back to the waiting room. Later that evening Lynette came by.

"Have you heard anything?"

"Not yet. Jackson said the baby is coming tonight. He's a nervous wreck, poor thing."

Audrey flipped through a three-month-old magazine. Susan pulled out her phone and caught up on her *Words with Friends* game. Lynette checked her messages. In the wee hours of the morning, Jackson came into the waiting room. His face was bright. All three jumped to their feet.

"He's here! Four pounds, seven ounces. Eighteen inches long. He's tiny, but he's breathing on his own. They've got him in an incubator."

"And Theresa? How is she?" said Susan.

"Exhausted, but thrilled. We're parents. I'm a father!"

"Congratulations," said Audrey. Susan and Jackson embraced Jackson in a group hug.

"What's his name?" said Audrey.

Jackson pulled out his phone and showed them all a his picture. "Meet my son, Ian Riley Simpson."

Chapter 32

Susan got to bed long past her usual bedtime, and in the morning, Mike had already gone to work by the time she woke up. She planned on stopping at the mall for a baby gift, visiting Theresa and the new baby in the hospital, then hitting the public library to dig for details on Maggie's office fire. Mike had left the coffee on for her, and if ever she needed it, it was today. *I'm too old to handle late nights anymore. I can't stop yawning.* Audrey was still asleep.

After finishing her oatmeal and reading through the newspaper, she set out for the mall, hitting it just as the lights inside Macy's turned on and an employee unlocked the door. The infant section was right inside the door. Fingering a miniature pink dress, she thought about how exciting it was when Lynette was expecting Annalise. *How nice it would be to have another grandchild. Annalise would be a great big sister.*

She waded through a sea of blue, picking out two preemie-sized onesies, striped overalls with a train embroidered on the front and a package of pastel-colored socks. *This is so much fun. If I don't get out of here, I'm going to buy half the store.* She drove to the hospital with the treasures.

There isn't a happier place than a maternity floor. Susan walked past doors adorned with pink and blue banners announcing "It's a boy," and "It's a girl." She passed a new mother in a flannel bathrobe shuffling down the hall and what looked like a new grandmother carrying a bouquet of pastel carnations bigger than her head. She walked around the circular corridor until she found Theresa's room.

"Congratulations, Mommy!" Theresa was sitting up in bed amidst an assortment of balloons and flowers. "How are you feeling? You look great."

"Happier than I even imagined," said Theresa. "I'm so relieved that Ian is going to be okay. I wasn't expecting him so soon."

"Good thing you've had his room ready for months. You let me know if you've forgotten anything, and I'll be happy to pick it up."

On her way out, Susan stopped at the nursery and got a peek of Ian in his incubator. Babies and kittens always make my heart melt. He's beautiful. Lots of dark hair like Theresa.

Time to tackle the next item on my to-do list .She made her way to the reference section of the public library. She discovered an article about the fire in Maggie's office, and it mentioned a "run of fortunately-timed fires in worthless properties." As she read, she discovered arson was suspected but never proven. She dug further and learned that the buildings were owned by the same business. Even more surprising, the business was an affiliate of the company that had dumped pollution into the water supply. In each case the owner received a large insurance payment worth more than the property warranted. She asked the reference librarian for help.

"You can find the details in public records. I'll show you." The librarian took the information from Susan and found copies of the deeds and real estate transactions. Susan scrolled through it as if sifting through river sludge for gold.

"Oh, my God, look at this!" The librarian peered over her shoulder. "Each of these transactions was handled by the same paralegal. Brooks Churchill!"

"It's a coincidence, but what does it mean?"

"Brooks Churchill oversaw the sale of each of these properties to the business which profited when they burned down."

Did Brooks burn down those properties, including Maggie's office? If so, what was his motivation? Money? Even so, he had no reason to kill Maggie. Susan was mystified.

She tried calling Lynette but was unable to reach her. Frustrated, she dropped by Jonathan's hotel.

"Jonathan, I think Brooks may have killed Maggie. I did some digging. Brooks was involved in the sale of properties to a business affiliated with the company that contaminated the water supply. Each of those properties coincidentally burned to the ground, yielding large insurance payouts."

"Brooks and Richard are friends. He had no reason to kill Maggie. Besides, he's the one spearheading Richard's defense. If he was the murderer, why on earth would he do that?"

"I don't know. Maybe he wanted to be sure Richard stayed in jail."

"Even if he's guilty of setting those fires, we can't link him to Maggie's murder."

"Is he here? Let's have a chat with him."

"I can't buy Brooks as a murderer." After listening to Susan's side over and over again, Jonathan reluctantly agreed to confront Brooks.

Brooks answered the door in sweats and a T-shirt. The television was on, and a half-eaten pizza was on the desk. "Susan, Jonathan, to what do I owe the pleasure? Come on in."

Susan began by asking about the properties. "I read that you were involved with the sale of several properties which ultimately burned down right around the time of Maggie's murder. I was curious. How did three pieces of real estate owned by the same company mysteriously burn down over a short course of time? It piqued my interest, and I wanted to see what you remembered."

"Ah, yes," said Brooks. "I was working as a paralegal. My specialty was real estate. I too thought it was fishy, but arson was never proven."

"All three were owned by a business associated with the company that dumped the pollution into the water supply." noted Susan.

Brooks sighed. Then he paced around the hotel room. "I didn't want to believe it, but as we cross suspects off our list, I'm inclined to believe the owner, Matt Cardwell, had something to do with Maggie's murder."

Jonathan said, "*Something* meaning what? You never mentioned him before now."

"Maggie's company sold Matt those properties. Maggie became suspicious after the second property burned down. I heard her on the phone. She threatened to turn him in to the police. Said she had some kind of proof that he had those properties torched for the insurance money. All the buildings were basically worthless. Matt Cardwell swept them up for next to nothing, then got the insurance payouts."

"Is Matt Cardwell still in town?" asked Jonathan.

Brooks took a bite of pizza. "I have no idea. Hadn't thought about him all these years."

Susan was silent. She couldn't help but ponder, *It's a small town. It makes sense Brooks worked on most of the real estate transactions here since it was his specialty. He's the second person who reported hearing Maggie argue and make a threat over the phone.* "I'll get Lynette to track him down," she said.

Chapter 33

Susan arrived home after dark. Mike and Audrey had already eaten dinner, and Annalise was asleep on the couch like a tired little angel. Audrey had agreed to watch Annalise for the day. Lynette debated sending her to Westbrook Developmental that morning since she'd been up half the night sniffling and rubbing her ear. Audrey overheard Susan and Lynette's phone conversation and jumped at the chance to spend time with her great-granddaughter.

"How's Annalise feeling?" asked Susan.

"She's got a bit of a runny nose, but other than that she seems fine. We had a great time. We read books, then took a walk through your neighborhood. I figured the fresh air would be good for her. Don't worry, I bundled her up with her jacket and blankets. It's been so long since I pushed a stroller!"

"She was talking a blue streak, like usual," said Mike. "I think it's just a cold."

Susan kissed Annalise, then made herself a frozen Lean Cuisine. She was starving. While she was eating, Lynette came by to pick up the baby, giving Susan the opportunity to tell her what she'd learned.

"I can search for Matt Cardwell in the morning," said Lynette. "I've been working on Axel's murder all day. I can't find anyone with motive to have killed him. It wasn't a robbery since his wallet was untouched and there were no witnesses. Very frustrating."

"Lynette, maybe Matt Cardwell killed him or had him killed to prevent him from clearing Richard. He was a big shot businessman here in town. He must still have ties. I'll bet he heard Axel was in town."

"I stopped by the hospital" said Susan. "The baby is so cute, even through glass and plastic. Theresa looks great."

"I stopped by during lunch. He is beautiful. Jackson is on cloud nine. I'm so happy for them." Annalise stirred on the couch. "I have to get her home. We'll talk in the morning."

Susan tossed and turned all night. Just when she was beginning to suspect Brooks, a new suspect pops up. She could picture the scenario. Businessman buys buildings for a song using Maggie as the real estate agent, then he torches them, or pays someone to do it for him, and collects the insurance money. Maggie finds out, so he kills her. *There was accelerant on the glove at the murder scene. Richard came home and surprised him, so he got out of there without having the chance to torch Maggie's house. Burning down her office was most likely a warning.*

Despite her restless night, Susan was awake at the crack of dawn. She had breakfast with Mike, then went to volunteer at the school. Janet greeted her warmly the moment she walked into the media center. It was nice to feel needed.

"So, how's the case going?" asked Janet. "I heard you talked to Anna Cabrini."

"Yes, and her father's death was a suicide, not a murder. We're working on a new lead. Maggie sold properties to a company related to the one we talked about. Those properties burned down."

"I remember that. There was talk of arson; the fires were under investigation. It was all over the news, but then they determined it wasn't arson."

"There were huge insurance payouts, all to the same owner—a guy named Matt Caldwell. He may have hired someone to do the dirty work. If it was arson and Maggie found out…"

"That person could be the killer. Have you talked to Matt Caldwell?"

"No, I'm waiting for Lynette to track him down."

"Good idea. You shouldn't be talking to a potential arsonist and murderer!"

Susan spent the morning in the media center, then started for home. On her way, Brooks called.

"Susan, great news. I located Matt Caldwell. He lives a few hours from here. Retired to an apple farm. Loves getting up on those branches and shaking down the fruit. I told Jonathan. Swing by the hotel, and we can make a road trip. I've been secretly working this angle for some time now. I didn't want to bring it up until we'd explored our other leads."

If Brooks was secretly working on finding Matt Caldwell, that explains his absence when we tried to find him the other night. *I hope he has something concrete.*

Again the adrenaline pumped. Susan made a U-turn and headed for the hotel. Jonathan and Brooks were waiting outside.

"I'll drive if you trust me with your car. I put directions into my phone." Brooks slid into the driver's seat. Susan volunteered to sit in the back.

It began to snow as they drove out farther into the country. Brooks was convinced Matthew Caldwell was the killer.

"Matt had a sleazy son-in-law, who was convicted of arson when he was a teenager. He got out of jail right around the time the properties started burning down. He tagged along with Matt Caldwell every time we signed a contract. Maggie suspected he was burning down the properties and confronted him. She was sure it was him who burned down her office."

"Then why didn't she go to the police?"

"She knew he was an expert. The fires were investigated, and arson was ruled out. Maggie needed proof. I think she found that proof, and that's what got her killed. There was accelerant on the glove found at the crime scene, right?"

"Yes, and DNA. If we can match it to his DNA, we're in business."

"I found his address. He and his wife live on the farm with Matt Caldwell."

"I should call Lynette," said Susan. Finally the pieces are coming together.

"Already did. She's meeting us there."

Susan dozed off in the backseat. When she awoke, Brooks was pulling into an abandoned gas station. "I have to check the directions. This doesn't seem right."

"Do you think they have a bathroom?" said Susan.

"Must have one. Try the side door. It looks open."

Susan made her way inside the gas station. It was dark, and it took her eyes a few minutes to adjust. The sound of her phone ringing made her jump.

"Hi, Lynette. I think we're lost, but we should be there soon."

"Where, Mom?"

"To Caldwell's farm." Suddenly Susan's stomach dropped. *Wait a minute. Jefferson Ramos said Caldwell had arthritis. How could he climb apple trees?*

"Mom, are you there? I need to tell you something. Caldwell is dead. Has been for years."

"But Brooks said he talked to him. We're going to meet him now. His son-in-law was convicted of arson. Brooks is sure it was him who set the fires and killed Maggie."

"Mom, you have to get out of there. I dug around and found out some information on Brooks. Remember how he suddenly left law school? He was failing out.

Blamed his professors. All this happened right before the law school burned down."

"Really?"

"Yes. He was suspected of starting the fire. That's why he was thrown out immediately. Iberton University didn't want bad publicity, so instead of charging him, they sent him packing."

Susan's brain felt like a merry-go-round. Fire in the dorm—Brooks was with Richard. Nina was killed—she was Brooks's ex. Richard didn't feel comfortable around fire—couldn't light a barbecue according to Audrey. Mr. Snow said they found lighter fluid near the dorm.

"Mom, you have to get out of there now. Are you alone?"

"No, Jonathan is with me." Maggie's office on fire. Brooks had a connection to each of the properties.

"Get out now. Make up an excuse you have to come back. Mom, Brooks owns a gun. It's the same caliber as the one that killed Axel Schumaker."

Axel Schumaker saw a green van in Maggie's driveway. Also saw a red sports car. Cynthia owned a green Miata. Brooks drove a red hippie van... Axel handed Jonathan the wrong color folder... said it happened all the time. He was colorblind! She felt sick to her stomach.

"Mom, he wanted to make sure Maggie's murder was pinned on Richard for good. Maggie found out he started the fires. We found her diary. Adair knew she kept one, and we found it in a safety deposit box after all these years."

"He's right outside with Jonathan. What if he doesn't believe me and figures out I know the truth?"

"Mom, do you know where you are?"

"We took the Thruway, then drove through country roads for what seemed like hours. I fell asleep. Wait, the gas station has a broken sign out front." She peeked through the window. "Art's Gas and Grill. Looks like it's been out of commission for years."

The door flew open. Susan jumped. Brooks was holding a gun to Jonathan's head. "Give me the phone. Now."

Susan's hand shook.

"Mom, Mom! What's going on? Is Brooks there now?"

Brooks said, "Give me the phone."

"Lynette, help! He has a gun!"

Brooks insisted, "Give me the phone right now."

Trembling, Susan dropped it to the ground. She could hear Lynette's voice until Brooks stepped on the phone, squashing it with his boot. She was shaking uncontrollably. "Jonathan, are you okay?"

"Don't worry about me." Brooks pushed the barrel of the gun right up against Jonathan's head.

"You had to meddle. You couldn't go with the flow, could you? I had to make sure Richard wasn't exonerated, but you kept finding new potential suspects. Richard is an evil man."

"But he didn't murder his wife. He doesn't deserve to be in jail. Why did you kill Maggie? Was it jealousy? Or did she find out it was you who set the fires back at the dorm, the law school, Maggie's office, Jonathan's office…"

"And the Caldwell properties. Collected a pretty penny for those. Maggie had to go snooping. She threatened to tell the police it was me. I had no choice."

Jonathan said, "Brooks, let's talk about this. No one has to know it was you. You're right. Richard is evil, and even if he didn't kill Maggie, he belongs in jail."

Susan took Jonathan's lead. "He's right. I visited Richard in jail. He has my mother wrapped around his little finger. If he gets out, he'll drain her of every penny and break her heart. I'm fine with leaving him there in prison." She shook her head in unison with Jonathan.

"Hmmm, Richard could stay in jail, and I'll go off to Aruba. Do they have extradition there?"

"No," said Jonathan. "You can live your life out on a sunny beach, and my brother will rot in jail."

"Let me think about this. I'll let you two go, I'll hop a plane, your detective daughter will keep her mouth shut, and we'll all live happily ever after."

"That's right," said Susan.

"You've got it," said Jonathan.

Susan felt her body relax. Maybe they'd get out of this after all. At this point she didn't care if Brooks escaped. She just wanted to get back home to her family and her cats. Brooks bent down and pulled a gas can from behind the counter, still with the gun aimed at Jonathan. He pushed them into the closet and locked the door.

"How stupid do you think I am? I was going to be a lawyer you know. Just like you, Jonathan. I coulda been a great one too."

Susan smelled gasoline and heard splashing outside the closet door. She banged on the door. "No, please Brooks. I have a husband and children and a granddaughter and a mother and…"

"Shut up. You'll see them again one day. In heaven." He snickered. Then Susan knew he was lighting a match. She heard a poof and then crackling sounds. She squeezed Jonathan's hand. "Brooks, don't do this. Please let us out. Don't do this."

Susan felt the door getting warm. She was sweating and shaking all at once.

Jonathan picked up a bucket and rammed it against the door. Then he tried jimmying the handle, which was getting hotter by the minute. "It's going to be okay, Susan. Someone will find us."

Susan knew the likelihood of being rescued was slim. The fire was spreading quickly. She could hear it. Soon she began coughing. "I can't take the smoke."

"Put your jacket over your mouth, and let's lie on the floor. There will be more oxygen there."

Susan worked her way to the floor and grabbed on to Jonathan. She thought about him dying with no family and said, "Jonathan, there's something important I have to tell you."

"Now's your chance."

"I have to tell you I…"

Suddenly Susan heard water rushing at the door. She screamed, "We're in here."

The door opened, and a fireman holding a hose helped her up.

"Are you okay, ma'am? Let's get you outside."

"Thank God. How did you find us?"

The fireman led her and Jonathan out of the gas station into Lynette's arms.

"Lynette, how did you find us?"

"The GPS on Brook's phone. We jumped in a helicopter, called the local police, and thank God we made it in time."

Jackson slapped cuffs on Brooks and read him his rights.

"Does Dad know we're safe? And Audrey?"

"They know. Tomorrow night we'll celebrate case closed."

"You can come to our house," said Susan.

"And I'll bring the food," said Jonathan.

Chapter 34

Susan set the table while Mike tossed the salad. Audrey pulled warm rolls from the oven.

"My mouth is watering," said Audrey. "There's nothing like fresh rolls." Borrowing Susan's frilly apron, she looked as though she'd stepped out of the pages of a 1960's *Good Housekeeping* issue. Ludwig rubbed against her legs. Johann poised to jump on the table, but Audrey shooed him away just in the nick of time.

Lynette and Jason arrived carrying lasagna. They'd picked up Jonathan on the way. He carried Annalise, who clung to his neck like a baby monkey.

"She sure loves you," said Susan. "It usually takes her a while to warm up to new faces, but you've got her in your back pocket."

Jonathan laughed. "I've always had a way with kids. This is one special girl here." He lifted her over his head and kissed her tummy. Annalise squealed, enjoying the attention.

I can't wait to tell him that Annalise is his great-granddaughter. I hope he isn't so angry about Audrey keeping it from him that he doesn't want to be part of our lives.

"Let's eat," said Lynette, "while it's still hot." She strapped Annalise into the high chair, then served the lasagna.

Scooping salad from the large glass bowl, Audrey said, "I can't wait till Richard gets out. He's going to come live with me in Florida. I can't wait for George to get to know him."

That will be interesting, thought Susan. *George already has Richard's number, just like I do. At least he'll be close by to keep an eye on things. My poor half-brother. Glad I'm living here and not there.*

Jason said, "I'm still not sure I understand why Brooks killed Maggie. I thought he and Richard were friends. How could he set him up like that?"

Susan said, "Brooks had a lifelong obsession with starting fires. He was jealous when Nina started seeing Richard back at Tarrington, so he set her dorm on fire, killing her."

"And he set the law library on fire when he was put on academic probation. The school knew he did it but, instead of prosecuting him, kicked him out and swept it under the rug. Bad publicity and all. That's when Richard offered him a job as a paralegal up in New York," said Jonathan.

Lynette cut more lasagna into bite-sized pieces for Annalise, who threw her sippy cup on the floor while becoming impatient for more food. Jonathan picked it up for her.

"Here you go, little buttercup." Annalise grabbed the handles.

Lynette continued, "He had a good thing going working with Maggie at her real estate business but got greedy. When one of Maggie's unscrupulous clients bought up worthless properties for next to nothing, he hired Brooks to burn them down, and the client collected the insurance money."

Jason said, "Why didn't he get caught? You're telling me all those fires, and no one put together that it was arson?"

Jonathan answered, "Brooks was good at what he did. He'd been playing with fire since he was a boy.

After all this went down, I started thinking back. He and Richard got into trouble with our parents on more than one occasion for setting fires in the backyard. My parents always assumed it was Richard's idea. I wish I'd remembered that earlier."

"He did get caught eventually—by Maggie. She put the pieces together and threatened to go to the police. He drove to her house intending to burn it down with her in it. That's why there was accelerant on the glove—the glove belonged to Brooks. Richard came home early, surprised him, so he had to hightail it out of there after he clobbered Maggie over the head." Lynette took another serving of lasagna. "Axel Schumaker saw Brooks's van in the driveway the night Maggie was killed, only he said he saw a green van. Brooks drove a red van. We now know that Axel was colorblind."

Annalise squirmed in her high chair. With Lynette's permission, Jonathan took her out and set her on his lap, where she quieted down and continued eating.

What a natural. He's a real gem, so much like the dad I grew up with. Annalise sure loves him.

"What about this Adair that Lynette mentioned?" said Jason.

"She and Maggie were estranged for a while, but Adair credits her sister with getting her back on track. Maggie's tough love got Adair to go to rehab and eventually nursing school. That's what Chief Charley told me."

"Chief Charley?" said Jason.

"Otherwise known as Chase, Adair's old boyfriend. Chief Charley says they've rekindled their relationship after all these years. He's taking a vacation in Atlanta over the holidays."

"Happy news all around," said Audrey.

"I heard Theresa and the baby are both home now. I'm going to stop by tomorrow to visit."

"Mom, I've never seen Jackson so happy."

"Babies have a way of doing that," said Susan. "Look at all the joy Annalise brings us."

Lynette got up and stood behind Jason, wrapping her arms around his neck. "There may just be a little more joy to go around."

Oh my God, have my prayers been answered? Is Lynette pregnant? "Lynette, are you pregnant?"

"Not exactly. But we are expecting a little bundle of joy. This little bundle is coming all the way from China. It's a girl!"

"What do you mean?"

"Jason and I decided we didn't want to go through all the infertility treatments and emotional ups and downs of trying to get pregnant again, so for some time now I've been researching adoption. We applied to an agency that handles adoptions from China and just found out we are approved. It could take months, maybe even a year, but we're going to have a little girl."

Susan jumped up and hugged her daughter. Mike, Audrey, and Jonathan followed suit.

"I'm so happy for you," said Audrey. "Adoption worked out so well for your mother. What a wonderful choice."

Mike said, "That settles it. Mom and I are going to sign up for Chinese language classes so we'll be ready."

"Dad, our baby will most likely be less than a year old. She'll learn English."

"No, Lynette. We have to keep her in touch with her roots—honor her heritage."

Chinese classes. Now that this mystery is solved, I'll need something to keep me occupied. Maybe I'll even take up Chinese cooking!

Lynette and Audrey cleared the table while Jonathan continued playing with Annalise.

He's leaving tomorrow. If I'm going to tell Jonathan he's my father, it's now or never.

"Jonathan, can I speak to you for a minute?" She led him out to the back porch, turning on the portable heater.

"What is it, Susan? Is everything okay?"

"I have to tell you something. Something important. As you know, Audrey is my birth mother. I only found out I was adopted after my mom died. It's taken some getting used to."

"Must have been quite a shock."

"It was. Audrey told me she'd lost track of my father. She never told him she was pregnant. She had no idea where he was."

"And?"

"She lied to me. That's why things have been so strained between us. I know now who my birth father is. Jonathan, it's you. You are my father." She was shaking as she said the words. She tried to read his expression. "Did you hear me?"

Jonathan hugged her tight, patting her back. "Yes, Susan."

"Are you shocked? Angry? This must be earth-shattering."

"Susan, the truth is..." He hugged her tighter. "I already knew..."

THE END

ABOUT THE AUTHOR

 Diane Weiner is a veteran public school teacher and mother of four children. She has enjoyed reading for as long as she can remember. She has fond memories of reading Nancy Drew and Mary Higgins Clark on snowy weekend afternoons in upstate New York and yearned to write books that would bring that kind of enjoyment to her readers. Being an animal lover, she is a vegetarian and shares her home with two adorable cats and a little white dog. In her free time, she enjoys running, attending community theater productions, and spending time with her family (especially going to the mall with her teenage daughter and getting Dairy Queen afterwards). *Murder is Legal* is Book 6 in her Susan Wiles School House Mystery series.